FL

## "I've been
## so wrong ab

Dominic slid his ~~fing~~ hair, tilting her face so that he could look into her eyes. "Can you forgive me?"

It wasn't a declaration of love or adoration, but it held a ring of genuine remorse that made her ache both for him and for herself.

"Kate, I want you so much. Eight years I've ached for you...dreamed about you, cursed the day I ever met you. You've become almost an obsession to me Kate, and now—"

"And now what?" she asked, suddenly afraid of placing too much meaning in what he was saying to her.

"And now I'm almost afraid to touch you," he admitted huskily.

Slowly she reached up and touched his mouth with her fingers.

"Don't be," she whispered.

**PENNY JORDAN** was constantly in trouble in school because of her inability to stop daydreaming—especially during French lessons. In her teens she was an avid romance reader, although it didn't occur to her to try writing one herself until she was older. "My first half-dozen attempts ended up ingloriously," she remembers, "but I persevered, and one manuscript was finished." She plucked up the courage to send it to a publisher, convinced her book would be rejected. It wasn't—and the rest is history! Penny is married and lives in Cheshire.

## Books by Penny Jordan

# PENNY JORDAN

## a man possessed

*Harlequin Books*

TORONTO • NEW YORK • LONDON
AMSTERDAM • PARIS • SYDNEY • HAMBURG
STOCKHOLM • ATHENS • TOKYO • MILAN

Harlequin Presents first edition March 1987
ISBN 0-373-10962-8

Original hardcover edition published in 1986
by Mills & Boon Limited

# CHAPTER ONE

'KATE, for goodness' sake, it's a dinner party I'm inviting you to, not a Roman orgy!'

With wry exasperation, Sue reflected that her husband John had been right when he said that Kate would dig her heels in and prove to be as intractable about refusing this invitation as she had been in refusing all their others.

She and Kate had been friendly ever since their High School days; they had grown up together, and yet despite that, there was a barrier between them now, that Kate used as a drawbridge, to pull up and hide herself behind.

Sue knew why, of course, and she sighed inwardly, reflecting how perverse and cruel fate could be. No woman gifted with Kate's looks and sensuality should live as she did, completely cutting herself off from almost all human contact. At least she had agreed now to put the farmhouse up for sale, Sue reflected. The land that had once gone with it was long gone, sold after Ricky's death to pay off his gambling and other debts. Kate refused to blame Ricky for the wasteland their marriage had been, but Sue's quick temper and loyalty to her friend were fired every time she thought about him. It was all very well for Kate to say that she was equally to blame; that she should never have married him. But she had been a naïve eighteen to his twenty-eight; still shocked by the sudden death of her father and the totally unexpected arrival into her life of the mother she had not seen since she was ten years old.

Perhaps Kate was right, and Ricky was not to blame; it had after all been Kate's mother who had been so eager for the marriage. The land Kate had inherited from her father had run alongside the farm Ricky had inherited from his grandfather, and he hadn't taken much persuading that in marrying Kate he would be gaining far more than a docile, biddable wife. Even then there had been rumours about his gambling, and Kate's mother must have known about them, but it had still not stopped her from marrying her daughter off to him, with what Sue, now a mother herself, recognised as extremely un-maternal haste. But then, at only seventeen and a half, Kate was still under age, and her mother would have had to take her back to the States with her, if she had not been able to leave her with Ricky.

Sue knew enough about Valerie Patton to know how unwelcome an addition a beautiful teenage daughter would have been to her Los Angeles lifestyle. Following her divorce from Kate's father, Valerie had resumed her acting career, landing a part in an American television 'soap', eventually giving up that role in order to take up the far more financially rewarding one of becoming Mrs Harold Patton the Third.

She had been frankly staggered when she saw Valerie at her ex-husband's funeral; she had looked barely half a dozen years older than her own teenage daughter, and almost as beautiful. But unlike Kate, Valerie's beauty was barely even skin deep; her charm as brittle and delicate as the mask that a clever plastic surgeon had fashioned on her face. No, there had been no room in Valerie Patton's life for a grown-up daughter, and so while she was still suffering from the shock of her father's death, Kate had been hustled into marriage with Ricky.

Only once in the ten years since then had Kate ever mentioned the subject of her marriage to Sue; and that had been six years ago, just after Ricky's death. What she had confided then had both appalled and stunned Sue. Even then Kate would not blame Ricky, claiming that she herself was as much to blame; that she had married him of her own free will believing herself in love with him, and that admission more than anything else had made Sue's sympathetic heart ache, especially now from the vantage point of her own maturity. What could a seventeen-and-a-half-year-old, who had only known the distant and ill-expressed love of a much older father, know of adult emotions? In Sue's opinion, if Kate had believed herself in love with Ricky, it had been because both Ricky himself and her mother had taken good care that she should do so. Although Kate had never confirmed it to her, Sue had a strong suspicion that knowing of Ricky's predilection for gambling, Valerie had offered him more than just her ex-husband's land when he married her daughter. After all, Valerie Patton was an extremely wealthy woman.

A soft, faintly mocking cough drew Sue back

from the past to the present. Kate was standing in
front of the window and the light from it framed
the darkly turbulent beauty of which she herself
was so unaware.

Once again Sue sighed. It was all such a waste.
Kate should be going out, meeting people,
enjoying life, not living here alone in this remote
farmhouse. She had tried again and again to get
her friend more interested in life ... in men, but
Kate had changed over the years. She was no
longer the shy, vulnerable adolescent she had
once been. In fact nowadays she was surprisingly
firm, self-possessed and stubborn; sometimes
maddeningly so, like now.

'Look, Kate, I promise you I'm not trying to
matchmake,' Sue told her firmly. 'I want you to
come to dinner with us, that's all.'

'Only with you and John?'

Humour curved her full bottom lip, her
densely blue eyes gleaming knowingly as Kate
looked back at her friend.

'No, not just John and me,' Sue admitted.
'There'll be others there ... But, Kate, can't you
see what you're doing to yourself?' She sounded
exasperated now, and she was. She had talked
this over with John again and again, and her
husband who was a G.P. in local practice agreed
with her that because of the isolation of her
home, and her habit of cutting herself off from
other people, Kate was in real danger of
becoming too solitary. 'You're young ... only
twenty-seven,' Sue persisted doggedly. 'You're
clever, beautiful ... Kate, you can't possibly
want to spend the rest of your life alone!'

Just for a moment a faintly brooding, haunted expression touched the blue eyes, and then they hardened to mocking flippancy as Kate responded teasingly, 'Why not?'

'Oh, you ...! Well, you're coming to this dinner party, even if it means driving out here to drag you back myself. You've got to start living again some time, Kate.'

Across the room their eyes met, and then suddenly, almost wearily, Kate gave in.

'Okay, I'll come,' she smiled wryly, 'who knows, I might be able to persuade one of your guests to buy the farm.'

Sue smiled. 'I'm glad you're selling it, although I know you've always loved it.'

'Yes, I know.' Kate smiled evenly at her and said with chilly truthfulness, 'I sometimes wonder if it was Ricky I married, or this place. I fell in love with it when I was six years old. I could just see the rooftops from our cottage. I can't afford to keep it on though, Sue—it costs a fortune to run.' She shrugged. 'I'm sure it's no secret locally how Ricky left me financially. What was left of the land had to go to meet his debts. Next winter the roof is going to need repairing. It's a listed building and can only be repaired with original or expensively hand-made roof tiles, and that's just the start of it ...'

'But what do you plan to do! Where will you go?'

'There's still the cottage,' Kate reminded her. 'It's been let as a weekend base to a couple from London for the past few years, but their tenancy runs out this year, and I've decided to move back there myself. It's plenty large enough for me after all, and it will be much cheaper to run.'

'And the money you get from this place, carefully invested, will bring you in enough to manage on, I suppose,' Sue mused, able to see the logic of what her friend was suggesting.

'It might do, but that's not what I've got in mind. I'm thinking of starting up my own business.'

Sue stared at her totally bemused for several seconds before exlaiming, 'Doing what?'

'Working in stained glass,' Kate told her calmly, amusement gleaming in her eyes as she surveyed her friend's stunned face. 'It was one of the crafts I studied at art school, and it fascinated me. I was only there six months, not long enough to learn very much, but I've been spending a couple of days each week over the last few months at a craft workshop in London learning more about it. The whole subject's one that intrigues me, and more and more markets are opening up for it—not just for restoration work in churches either.'

'But . . . but you've never said a word!'

Kate shrugged and then smiled. 'Until now there was nothing to say. Although I've enjoyed what I've been doing, until Harry suggested we went into partnership last week, it never really occurred to me that it might be a way in which I could make a living.'

'Harry!' The stunned, almost inarticulate way in which Sue repeated the name of her mentor and proposed partner made Kate grin mischievously.

'Don't get excited,' she cautioned, chuckling. 'He's fifty, happily married and a grandfather.'

'But, Kate——! I'm amazed . . . you've been making all these plans and never said a word!'

Kate could tell that her friend was hurt and hurriedly made amends.

'To be honest with you, Sue, until Harry mentioned us going into partnership last week, I hadn't thought of what I was doing as anything other than an enjoyable hobby, but now that he has mentioned it, I really feel that it's something I want to do. Of course we're only talking about it at this stage, but Harry's very enthusiastic. He likes my designs and he's keen for me to develop that side of my work.'

Sue sat down in a chair and stared up at her. 'Kate, I'm so pleased. This is just what you need to take you out of yourself. I'm sorry you've got to sell the house, of course, but it's time you had a fresh start.'

'Mmm . . . maybe. But keep it to yourself, would you, Sue? My plans are far too tentative at the moment to become the subject of village gossip.' Kate made a rueful moue. 'You know what this place is like.'

'Only too well! Don't worry, I shan't breathe a word.'

The grandfather clock in the hall suddenly struck the hour and Sue jumped up, grimacing. 'God, is it that time? I've got to pick the kids up from school in half an hour. I'd better go . . . but before I do, I want your promise that you'll come to my dinner party.'

'You've got it.'

'Good, because I meant what I said, you know. I'll come and drag you away from this place forcibly if you try and wriggle out of it now.'

'Oh, yeah!' Glancing from the vantage point of her five-feet-eight to her friend's petite five-foot-nothing, Kate grinned, reviving a taunt from their mutual schooldays as she teased, 'You and whose army?'

Ten minutes later, bowling down the lane in her small car, heading in the direction of the village, Sue reflected warmly that at long last Kate was showing some signs of rejoining the human race. She couldn't wait to get home and share her pleasure with her family. Her husband was almost as fond of Kate as she was herself, and her widowed mother loved Kate almost as a second daughter. It was so good to see her smiling again; reverting to the lovely laughing girl she had been before her father's death, and then again, if only briefly, in those weeks before her marriage. How long after that marriage had it been before she stopped smiling? A month . . . six weeks? Over and over again Kate had denied that her unhappiness was Ricky's fault, but in the shocked aftermath of his death she had broken down completely and admitted to her what a travesty their marriage had been.

Sexually Ricky had been completely indifferent to her; had made love to her less than half a dozen times, always perfunctorily, from what Sue had been able to gather from Kate's weepy outpourings; and then once they had been married a couple of months, never touching her, but turning instead for sexual pleasure to a

succession of girl-friends. He had been with one
of them when he died in a horrifying head-on
crash with another car. Kate had wanted to
divorce him, she had confided, but she had been
too ashamed of admitting to anyone what a
travesty their marriage was to do anything about
it.

What her friend had experienced would be
enough to put any woman off the male sex for
life, Sue admitted, but although Ricky had
apparently constantly jeered at her for being
sexually cold, that was not how Sue saw her
friend. On the contrary, she had always thought
there was an aura of warm sensuality about Kate
. . . an air of womanliness and warmth, spiced
with sexuality, and she knew that her husband
John agreed with her. Even so . . . physical
rejection from one's husband must be a terrible
burden to carry . . .

Although she wasn't aware of it, as she stood by
the drawing-room window looking out on to the
mellow countryside Kate's thoughts were following a similar path to her friend's, although it
was not the bitterness of the burden of her
husband's rejection that was occupying her
thoughts, but that of another man.

Strange how, even now, after all this time,
eight years in fact, that memory still had the
power to torment her. She sighed, and tried to
push it away, turning her back on the scenery
outside and turning instead to survey the familiar
surroundings of her home, but that was a
mistake.

Nothing had changed in this room in over ten
years. It was still the same now as it had been
when she came to the house as a new bride.
Although she hadn't known it at the time, the
décor had been chosen by one of Ricky's girl-
friends. Whoever she was, she had had excellent
taste, Kate mused, her glance taking in the soft
lemony-gold washed walls and ceiling; the dark
stained beams which were part of the original
Elizabethan house. From the parish records they
knew that this house had once belonged to a
prosperous buccaneer, who had made his money
with Drake, and who had bought this land with
the Queen's goodwill, building a home on it for
the bride he had brought here from London.

A soft blue-grey velvety carpet covered the
floor, the cottagey atmosphere of the drawing-
room reinforced by the two large sofas upholstered in a beautiful Colefax and Fowler print
of blues and greys on a soft yellow background.
An antique ladies' writing desk was set against
one wall beneath an attractive group of prints.
The room retained an open fireplace and was
large enough to take a collection of antique
occasional tables, and a couple of easy chairs
upholstered in soft yellow fabric to contrast
slightly with the florals of the sofas. Matching
curtains hung at the windows at either end of the
room, the whole effect a careful blending of
colours that harmonised, seemingly casual and
slightly shabby and yet epitomising a country
house style of furnishing that was wholly English.
Which made it all the more disruptive that she
should be able to so easily imagine standing

within this background a man who was most definitely not the slightest bit English—at least not in looks—and one, moreover, who had spent no more than a mere weekend at most here. And yet it was easier to recapture his image than it was to recapture Ricky's. But then, of course, the rejection she had suffered at Dominic Harland's hands had been far more savagely painful than that she had known with Ricky.

She shivered, suddenly cold despite the afternoon sun pouring into the room. Even now she couldn't bear to think about that weekend.

But perhaps she should, she told herself hardily; perhaps it was time she stopped hiding away from the past and faced up to it. She was after all about to make a new start in life . . . a fitting point at which to give one final look at the past and then shut it away for ever.

Almost dreamily she walked into the large hall, glancing automatically up to what had originally been the minstrels' gallery and what was now the landing. He had been standing up there the first time she saw him. She had been in bed when he arrived . . . had known nothing about him until Ricky, whom she had not expected home that weekend, told her that he was an old friend whom he had met in London and invited down for the weekend.

Numbly Kate tore her attention away from the gallery, shocked by the unexpected pallor of her own face as she caught sight of it in the mirror hanging on the hall wall. She looked drained of all colour, her hair stark black, although in reality it was very dark brown, the curling thick mass of it in stark contrast to her face, as though somehow her hair had drained all the colour and energy from her skin. Even her mouth looked pale, almost bloodless, only her eyes possessing colour.

Her colouring was Irish, her father had once told her, which was why he had chosen to call her Kate, but Kate could see no beauty in her vibrantly sensual colouring; she would have preferred to have been blonde like her mother. Ricky had always preferred blondes too. The girl he had died with had been blonde ... bleached apparently, but blonde nevertheless.

Slowly Kate went upstairs, her feet automatically finding the shallow indentations on the stairs made by the feet of many generations. One of the things she loved most about the house was its age.

She found it soothing to remind herself that these walls and rooms had seen every facet of human life both happy and miserable, and in the past it had often given her a sense of perspective on her own problems to think of this.

Once upstairs she made for her bedroom and sat down on the edge of the bed. It was not the room she had shared with Ricky during their marriage. She went in there these days only when she had to. Ricky had insisted that she continue to share the huge fourposter with him even when he had made it plain that he had no interest in her as a woman—how galling that had been, to know that her husband, who would turn in the street and look lustfully at almost every girl who walked past him, had absolutely no sexual interest in her.

She closed her eyes, automatically letting the past wash over her, remembering how confused and uncertain she had been after her father's death. Her mother might have pushed her into Ricky's arms, but she hadn't had to push too hard. The trouble was that she had been in desperate need of someone to love and be loved by in return. Ricky had been attractive enough to make any naïve girl's heart beat faster; tall, fair-haired, and indolently languid in a way which Kate had misinterpreted as being sophisticatedly exciting—she had been all too eager to believe herself in love with him.

Her full lips twisted slightly. God, what a fool she had been! Well, she had soon learned the truth. Ricky had refused to take her away on honeymoon, claiming that he was too busy, but she soon realised that Ricky used those words to cloak his heavy gambling. He had gone gaming the night they were married, leaving her alone in the house after the few guests who had attended their register office wedding had gone. He had come back late—and drunk. Weeks later when she had accused him of this he had sneered at her in open contempt and told her that that was the only way he had been able to bring himself to make love to her. Although she hadn't known it when they married he had been heavily involved with someone else, a woman whose tastes were much more in accord with his than her own.

It was when, after a tearful fight, she had accused him of not loving her that he had told her this, and much more besides, jeering at her for ever believing he might have done.

He had never wanted her, he told her then, and never would; she was too cold ... too inexperienced. No, the reason he had married her was because the addition of her father's land to his own had made it much easier for him to raise a mortgage on the land, and that plus the fact that her mother had been willing to pay him to take her off her hands had made marriage to her an attractive proposition.

They had been married exactly two months when he told her that, and at first she had been too shocked to take it in.

Convinced that his hurtful words were just born out of temper, she had made several clumsy attempts to approach him and to bridge the gap between them, but he had rebuffed her so callously that she was soon forced to realise what he had said was the truth and that he did not desire her as his wife in any physical sense at all.

At first she had been too shocked to think of divorce; to do anything other than live through each agonising day as best she could. The discovery that he did not love her, coming so soon after the blow of her father's death, numbed her to such an extent that for months she had simply drifted through life.

But then two years after she and Ricky were married had come that dreadful, fateful weekend when she had met Dominic Harland.

Ricky had arrived home late one Friday evening with him.

Kate had been in bed when they arrived. The sound of Ricky's car had woken her and she had gone out on to the landing in just her cotton nightdress, not expecting Ricky to have anyone with him. He had not been home at all the previous night and she was rigid with tension and anguish, only registering the other man's presence when he stepped out from behind her husband. The light on the landing threw his profile into strong relief and she had literally gasped out loud, stunned by the masculine perfection of his features. Honey-gold skin stretched tautly over strong bones, tawny-gold eyes, the colour of a lion's pelt, stared mockingly into her own, thick black hair curling down over the collar of his shirt.

Even in her ignorance and innocence Kate had recognised the powerful sexual aura of the man, and a curious, twisting sensation curled through her body, making her eyes widen and her lips part as she stared down into his face like someone possessed. Her heartbeat quickened, her whole body pulsing with a deep, aching sensation hard to define. As she watched, transfixed, the hard male mouth twisted, the golden eyes narrowing, hardening, disengaging from her own with cool indifference making her uncomfortably aware of the long schoolgirlish plait of her hair, and the little girlish cotton nightdress she was wearing. No doubt his women wore silks and satins to bed; their appearance as sophisticated as his own. As she stumbled back to the bedroom she had a momentary and tormenting mental picture of his naked body, tanned and hard; very sure and knowing as it reached out to claim the filmy image of a woman, in the act of love.

Her skin hot with shame, Kate dived into bed

and curled up beneath the bedclothes. There must be something wrong with her, thinking like that about a complete stranger. There *was* something wrong with her, she decided distractedly minutes later as an uncomfortable heat pervaded her body, followed by a tight, coiling tension. She could hear the two men moving about in the adjacent bedroom. The door opened and closed, she heard footsteps along the landing and then her door opened and Ricky came in.

She knew better now than to make any approach to him. He undressed quickly, throwing his clothes on to the floor before heading for their bathroom. He was gone for over half an hour, but when he returned Kate was still awake. She felt the bed depress as he got in beside her, turning his back on her. She closed her eyes, but it was not her husband's image that danced tormentingly behind her shuttered lids. It was Dominic Harland's.

And that was how it had begun, Kate thought wryly, shaking herself free of the past and opening her eyes, knowing that she did not have the courage to take herself back through that entire weekend. God, the humiliation of what had heppened! It scorched and burned her even now, far, far more than any rejection she had endured at Ricky's hands. Of course, it had all been her own fault. She ought to have realised the moment she set eyes on him what manner of man he was. Certainly not the type who could ever be interested in a shy, naïve girl such as she had been. But she had been so desperate then to

prove that she was a woman that she had not seen
that. She had only seen that he was a man who
aroused within her desire and in whose arms she
could wipe out the humiliation of her husband's
lack of interest in her.

She laughed bitterly. Heavens, how stupid she
had been! But that was all in the past now. The
grandfather clock struck four, and she remembered that she had promised to telephone
Harry and give him her decision about going into
partnership with him.

It was only this afternoon talking to Sue that
she had realised what she intended to do.
Squaring her shoulders slightly, she went downstairs. It was time she made a fresh start, put the
past behind her once and for all and what better
way could there be to do that than to embark on a
new career?

As she dialled the number of Harry's workshop,
she smiled slightly to herself. It was almost two
years since they had first met now. She had gone
to London on business to see Ricky's solicitor.
Following her husband's death she had discovered
that he had considerable debts outstanding to
various gambling establishments, and although
the solicitor had advised her that she was under
no legal obligation to clear them, she had insisted
that she wanted to do so. With the sale of what
had been her father's land, she had been able to
clear the last of these outstanding amounts, and it
had been that that took her to London.

With a free afternoon at her disposal she had
wandered through Covent Garden, pausing to
study the goods on sale on the wide variety of

stalls, and it was there that her interest in stained glass had been rekindled when she spotted an attractive selection of window ornaments on sale on one of the stalls.

Seeing her interest, the girl who ran the stall had told her about the artisans' workshop which had recently been established in London's dockland to give craftsmen an opportunity to develop their work, and she had gone on to invite Kate to go back there with her to see the workshops for herself.

Normally very reticent about involving herself with strangers, on impulse Kate had accepted her invitation, and it had been at the workshop that she first met Harry. Harry was their mentor and teacher; Lucy, the girl who had invited Kate back with her, explained that it was Harry who taught them the intricacies and skills of working in stained glass, and on hearing his name, the tall, bearded man had ambled over to introduce himself and to chat to Kate.

Other craftsmen besides the glass workers shared the same premises, and Harry had elected to take Kate on a brief tour. She had watched fascinated as she saw her contemporaries engrossed in such traditional skills as gilding, marbling, marquetry and a wide variety of other crafts, but it was the glass work that fired her imagination.

What she had intended to be a brief courtesy visit in response to Lucy's invitation lasted well into the late afternoon. They were a very friendly crowd, most of them around her own age or younger, with a smattering of much older tutors, who like Harry were keen to pass on their own skills to a younger generation.

'It's their interpretation of the skills we teach them that we find so stimulating,' Harry told her enthusiastically. 'They're young and their ideas are fresh. It's fascinating, and an education for us to see what they can do.'

While he was talking Kate was absorbed in watching a young man deftly shaping the lead to hold the glass he was working on, and seeing her, Harry smiled, touching her arm to say disarmingly, 'You're dying to try it for yourself, aren't you?'

'It fascinates me,' she admitted. 'We touched on the subject very briefly on the arts course I took, but I hadn't thought of it as having any modern application.'

'Mmm ... you thought of it as being applicable only to church windows, that sort of thing. Well, it's a common enough mistake, although nowadays many young architects and designers are becoming far more aware of its possibilities. Only the other week young Rob over there finished a commission for a renovated Victorian conservatory. It really was beautiful, a trail of climbing roses all along one glass wall. The small bits and pieces, the window hangings, plant containers, that sort of thing, they're the bread and butter, but the jam is in the new commissions we're getting, and we're getting more and more all the time.' He paused and looked at her consideringly. 'If you're really interested, why don't you come to my classes?'

Kate had shaken her head, instinctively

retreating from the suggestion in the way that she retreated from everything. Her life with Ricky had left painful scars, and the loneliness of her life which Sue saw as a handicap she saw as protection, but less than a week later she found herself on the London train once more with the intention of taking Harry up on his offer.

Since then, her friendship with Harry, and to some lesser extent with some other members of the workshop, had grown, and six months ago her first commission was accepted—a feature window panel for the new, prestigious office block of a three times winner of the Queen's Award to Industry, whose go-ahead young architect wanted a modern design to include both these and some indication of the company's business. Since this was the rapid transportation of parcels and goods, Kate had chosen a bird motif, the swift, and when Harry told her that her design had been accepted she had been almost speechless with delight.

Quite early on in their relationship she had discovered that Harry lived only twenty miles away from her. She had met his wife and two grown-up daughters and their children and now felt quite comfortable in the small family circle.

Harry's suggestion that they set up in business together had come entirely out of the blue. It would be a challenge for both of them to move outside the protective security of the craft centre, but it was a challenge that suddenly she was eager to accept.

Harry was convinced that her design for Howard Transport would bring in further commissions, and in addition to that, Harry himself had been offered a contract with the Church authorities to make repairs and care for the windows in parish churches in a fifty-mile radius of Dorchester, which would bring in enough work to keep them both working steadily in the early months of their partnership.

Their work would not make them millionaires, Harry had told her that, but it would be stimulating and a constant challenge. Already she was a regular visitor to the Victoria and Albert Museum, avidly studying everything she saw, her busy mind drinking in all that was best of the period and working out how she could translate it into modern-day designs.

Liz, Harry's wife, answered the phone and chatted to Kate for a few minutes before summoning her husband.

When he took over the receiver, Kate had a few seconds' panic. Was she acting too impulsively? She would have to sell the house to raise her share of the capital they would need to set themselves up and give themselves a safe margin of working capital, and despite everything that had happened she was still deeply attached to her home . . . but then how long could she keep it on anyway? As she had said to Sue earlier, the roof needed attention . . . Taking a deep breath, she banished her panic, and calmly told Harry of her decision.

Hary was predictably delighted.

'That's great! I'll make us an appointment at the bank . . . and how about coming round for dinner on Saturday to celebrate?'

'I'd love to, but I can't. I've already promised to have dinner with an old friend.'

The words were out before Kate realised what a first-rate excuse he had given her to pass on Sue's dinner party, but it was too late to recall them now, Harry was chuckling and telling her that it was high time she started going out a bit. Harry knew nothing about her past life, other than that she had been widowed young. She never mentioned Ricky other than in passing, and neither Harry nor his family ever questioned her about him. It was so much easier to adopt the mantle of a young woman, widowed tragically young, who had loved and been loved by her dead husband, than to live with the truth, which was, no doubt, why she was sometimes so prickly with Sue, she thought guiltily.

After all, it was not Sue's fault that she had confided in her, and like the true friend that she was, Sue had never raised the subject with her since. She had needed the catharsis of confiding in someone, so why now did part of her resent the fact that she had?

Shrugging aside thoughts far too deep for such a mellow summer afternoon, Kate opened the french windows and went outside.

The sunken brick patio, with its terracotta pots of plants and traditional wrought iron furniture, had been designed by Ricky's mother, and Kate often wondered wistfully if things might have been different if she had known Ricky's parents. They had died when he was four years old, killed in a plane crash, leaving Ricky to be brought up by his grandfather.

Beyond the patio lay the smooth greenery of the lawns with their cottage garden herbaceous borders. A brick path in the same soft earthen colours as the house and patio meandered through the lawns and through a rose-smothered brick wall to the enclosed area which had originally been a kitchen garden and which was now a brick-paved sun-trap complete with pool and fountain and some extremely large and lazy koi carp.

Kate loved the garden almost as much as she loved the house. She found working in it relaxing and therapeutic. She had spent almost the entire summer following Ricky's death busy in it, exhausting herself physically to the point where she could drop into bed at night and fall fast asleep.

Those had been worrying days; days during which she had finally grown up, when she realised the extent of the debts her husband had left . . . the extent of his infidelity to her. Days when she had finally come to realise that the blame for the failure of their marriage was not hers alone . . . that she was no more to blame for the fact that Ricky was not attracted to her than he had been.

She walked through the garden and sat down by the pool, watching with a slight smile as the greedy carp surfaced, waiting to be fed. As she watched them, in her mind's eye, she pictured the scene done in stained glass. The goldfish forgotten, she got up and hurried back to the house, making for the study.

Time passed without her being aware of it as

she worked, stopping only when the light started to fade, astonished to discover how long she had been sitting at her desk. She even felt hungry. She grimaced faintly. Sue was always telling her that she was too thin. It was true she was a little on the slender side, but food rarely interested her.

Once things had been different. In the early days of her marriage she had eaten for comfort, thoroughly confused by Ricky's attitude towards her. She had never been fat, but it was probably fair to say that she had been a little chunky. She frowned, dismissing the too intrusive memories waiting to surface, and got up flexing her lithe body, encompassed by a sense of wellbeing as she looked down and studied the work she had done.

# CHAPTER TWO

'AND if you want a lift tonight . . .'

Kate interrupted Sue's busy flood of words to say calmly, 'No, I'll drive myself over.'

'In that death-trap you call a car?' Sue was plainly horrified. 'Honestly, Kate, it's barely roadworthy!'

'It passed its M.O.T.,' Kate responded mildly. It was true that her ancient Mini was on its last legs, but she couldn't afford to change it and, living as remotely as she did, some form of personal transport was essential. She was easily ten miles away from the nearest village—ten miles down narrow, empty country lanes at that.

'I can easily arrange for you to be picked up,' Sue persisted, but Kate remained adamant. She knew her friend of old. Although Sue insisted that she had no intention of matchmaking, Kate suspected that whoever got the chore of picking her up would be male and unattached, and as embarrassed and disgruntled as she would be herself by Sue's so obvious machinations.

She knew that her friend meant well, but every time she tried to pair her off, Kate was reminded of the failure that her marriage had been and it left her feeling as though she were incapable of attracting anyone by herself . . . that she was somehow intrinsically lacking as a woman. It was a fear that rose up to haunt her

with monotonous regularity. She had told herself
that it didn't matter that sexually she was
undesirable. She was perfectly happy with her
life as it was, but deep down the knowledge still
nagged at her ... taunting her, and that was
something she had never confided to anyone.
And it wasn't as though it were only Ricky who
had rejected her. Shivering slightly, she walked
into the kitchen and made herself a cup of coffee.
After the lazy summer warmth of the last few
days, this morning's rain was disheartening, even
if the garden did need it. She had no idea what to
wear for Sue's dinner party. Although her friend
had not changed over the years, her circle of
friends had, and included several very sophisticated London-based couples who found the village
so conveniently just off the M4 an ideal spot in
which to have a weekend cottage.

The contents of her wardrobe could hardly
rival the clothes worn by women accustomed to
shopping in Knightsbridge, she told herself
ruefully, and then almost immediately was
struck by the strangeness of her thought.
Normally her appearance was the last thing to
worry her when she was invited out. Shrugging
the thought aside, she went upstairs to see what
she could find.

Her clothes were serviceable rather than
attractive. After Ricky's death there had been no
money to spare for such fripperies even if she had
wanted them, and her normal garb consisted of
jeans, shirts and jumpers.

She frowned slightly as her fingers touched her
few summer dresses, most of them relics from the

early days of her marriage when she had naïvely
hoped to impress Ricky with the cheap chain-
store clothes she had bought locally in Dorchester.
She hadn't known then that he was accustomed
to far more attractively and sophisticatedly
dressed women than she could ever hope to be.
Her frown deepened as she touched a dress as yet
never worn. It had arrived the Christmas before
last, a large brown parcel with American stamps,
a Christmas present from her mother. The first
one she could ever remember receiving since her
parents' divorce, she thought wryly now, fingering the rich deep pink silk fabric. Why her
mother had sent her such an obviously expensive
and unsuitable gift was a complete mystery to
her, and after one look at it she had consigned it
to the back of her wardrobe, knowing she would
never have either the self-confidence or the
occasion to wear such an outfit. But now things
had changed, she thought, fingering the fabric
absently. If the secondhand *Vogues* Sue passed on
to her were anything to go by, even the most
simple dinner party now demanded sophisticated
dressing, and the prospect of her new career had
given her a self-confidence she had never
expected to have.

Impatiently she tugged the dress off its hanger
and held it in front of her. She had never even
tried it on, but one glance at the label had made
her decide that her mother had indulged herself
in malicious amusement in sending her a size ten
dress when, on the last occasion they had met,
Kate would have had difficulty in getting into a
size twelve.

Now, however, things were different, and the draped, wrapover style of the dress meant that the bodice would easily accommodate what she personally considered to be her rather over-full breasts.

Against the rich intensity of the silk her skin took on a matt creamy tone that emphasised the sultry darkness of her hair; the image she could see in the mahogany pier-glass at once familiar and yet unfamiliar, tantalisingly hinting at another Kate, and one moreover who looked as though she could be as turbulent and passionate as Shakespeare's vividly drawn Shrew. Impatiently she dismissed her thoughts as ridiculous. Cool control, that was what she aimed to portray, it was safer ... made her less vulnerable. Annoyed with herself, she threw the dress down on to the bed. She would have to wear it, she had nothing else suitable, and after all, who was going to notice her? Certainly not whatever poor male Sue had picked out for her, for despite her friend's promise, Kate knew enough about her to suspect that Sue had picked someone out.

Fifteen miles away in the comfortable Edwardian house that had once been a vicarage Sue was frowningly concentrating on what her husband was saying. John Edwards was a large, placid man who was a good doctor and a compassionate one. He could tell by his wife's face that she didn't like what he was saying, but he still continued mildly, 'It isn't on, Sue, and Kate will be furious ... you know that.'

'But it isn't my fault, it was the Bensons who asked if they could bring him. He's a close friend of theirs, apparently, more or less completely on his own in London ... what could I say?'

'Mmm ... well, Kate won't see it that way. It would have been much better if you'd explained the situation to her. She'll take one look at him and immediately she's going to think the obvious—that he's someone you've invited specifically to partner her, and you know how sensitive she is about that sort of thing.'

'Mmm. Honestly, John, it almost breaks my heart. It's such a waste ... She's so beautiful, but she behaves as though she's the original Ugly Sister.'

'I know. Ricky Hammond has one hell of a lot to answer for.' John got up and put an arm round his wife's shoulders. 'I know you only want to help her, Sue, but you can't. God alone knows what kind of psychological damage Hammond and her mother between them did to her, but it certainly can't be put right by arranging dinner party partners for her.'

'Then what will put it right?'

'I don't really know. It sounds trite, but all I can think of is good old-fashioned love, and Kate's so withdrawn I doubt she could ever allow herself to believe any man could love her.'

'How could he do that to her, John?' Sue asked her husband miserably. 'How could Ricky marry her and then treat her like that?'

'Men like Hammond who are driven by an obsession, whether it's drink, drugs or gambling, don't function in the same way as the rest of us.'

'Mmm ... If I ring Kate now and tell her that the Bensons are bringing a spare man, ten to one she'll refuse to come.'

'Okay, but be prepared for fireworks,' her husband warned her with a grin. 'Kate won't like it. Who is this man anyway?'

'I don't know his name. Vera Benson simply rang up last night and asked if they could bring him along. Apparently he's in the same line of business as her husband—merchant banking, although at the moment he's based in New York. Vera said he was thinking of transferring his main business to London, something about world time differences working more efficiently for him in London than they do in New York.'

'Mmm ... a lot of the big money men are transferring their business to London. Because of the new sophisticated communications systems it means that they can take advantage of the fact that, during the British working day, they can get in touch with both New York and Hong Kong during their working days, which gives them an immediate advantage.'

John grinned at his wife's astounded expression and admitted wryly, 'I read it in the *Sunday Times* magazine. If the Bensons' friend is one of these money men, chances are he'll be a real high-flier. Most of them are burned-out by the time they're thirty.'

'Oh, yeah? Did you read that in the *Sunday Times* as well?'

'Yep.' His smile was unrepentant, as he added comfortingly, 'It sounds as though he isn't going to be Kate's type at all. If I know anything about these big business men he'll spend most of the evening talking with Benson, so with any luck Kate won't realise you're trying to palm him off on her.' He broke off as he saw the frown pleating his wife's forehead and enquired, 'Now what's the matter?'

'What? Oh ... if he's as important as all that, he's not going to think much of the simple meal I was planning to serve. I wonder if it's too late to ...'

'Yes,' John told her firmly. 'Whatever it is you're planning to change, don't. He'll probably appreciate simple fare for a change. For goodness' sake, Sue, stop worrying. It's giving you grey hairs,' he teased, watching as his wife abandoned her concern over the menu to rush over to the mirror to stare at her still-bright blonde hair.

Half-past eight was the time Sue had specified for her arrival, and knowing that she needed to allow a good three-quarters of an hour to drive to Sue's home, at half-past six Kate abandoned the work she was doing and went upstairs to run a bath.

At half-past seven she was ready to slip into her dress. She paused to check her make-up first, wondering if the deep pink glossy lipstick was too much. She had a natural eye for colour, and although she didn't wear make-up very often, tonight she had found it surprisingly easy to apply. Just a touch of dark blue eyeshadow brought out the intense depth of her eyes, blusher highlighting the cheekbones which gave her face its distinctive definition. The fullness of her mouth beneath its careful coating of lipstick was almost gypsyish, as was the untamed thickness of her hair worn long now as opposed to the short, almost boyish cut her mother had chosen for her just before her marriage.

She picked up the dress and put it on, securing the two buttons that fastened it at the waist. It fitted her surprisingly well, the wide stiffened belt that went with it emphasising the smallness of her waist, the silk hissing softly as she walked across the room to put on her shoes—a rather old pair of black high-heeled sandals which were the only suitable footwear for the dress that she had.

In them she would probably tower over most of the other guests at the dinner party, including the men, she thought wryly, eyeing her five foot eight frame with familiar dislike.

The rain had stopped, and as she stepped outside she breathed in deeply, savouring the fresh, clean smell of wet grass and earth. She was so lucky to live here . . . to have the lifestyle that she did, and even though she had to part with the house, she still had the cottage.

There had been a letter for her in the post this morning from her solicitor confirming that the lease was now terminated. Tomorrow she must go down to the cottage and look over it, and then she would have to put the house on the market for sale.

Sighing faintly, she slid into the driver's seat of her ancient car and started the ignition. As always it was several minutes before the little car coughed and spluttered into life. This evening for some reason in fact, it seemed more reluctant than ever to start, and even once it had, the engine ran in a hesitant, uncertain fashion that made Kate guiltily aware that it was some months since she had last had it serviced.

Because she felt reluctant to push her car too hard, she arrived later than she had anticipated and there were three unfamiliar cars already parked in the Martins' generous drive before her.

She stopped her car and got out, cursing herself for arriving late. She would have preferred to arrive first so that she could study her fellow guests without feeling that they were scrutinising her. Now it might seem almost as though she had deliberately delayed in order to make an entrance.

Sue opened the door for her, her eyes widening in stunned appreciation of her dress.

'Kate, you look fantastic!' she enthused, hugging her. 'Where on earth did you get that?'

'My mother sent it to me a couple of Christmases ago.' She grimmaced faintly. 'I hope I'm not going to be overdressed.'

'In that?' Sue grinned mischievously at her. 'I doubt that any man would think so. It's really quite sexy . . .' She could have bitten her tongue when she saw Kate's wary, troubled expression, and quickly hurried her towards the drawing-room, whispering as she did so, 'The others have all arrived. The Hugheses and the Dentons came together, but . . .' She broke off as they reached the open drawing-room door, standing back so that Kate was forced to precede her through it.

The Martins' drawing-room was as familiar to her as her own and so she was free to concentrate

her attention on her fellow guests. Two couples
stood by the window chatting, and Kate vaguely
recognised them from Sue's Christmas cocktail
party. One of the men was a consultant based at the
local hospital and the other man was something in
hospital administration. The quartet saw her and
smiled in her direction. Nothing to worry about
there—two comfortably married middle-aged
couples. A little of her apprehension melted and the
tension down her spine eased slightly.

'Kate, come and meet Vera and Ian Benson.
They've bought The Grange . . .'

The couple Sue wanted to introduce her to
were standing by the fireplace, and John stood
behind them, his head turned away from her,
obviously speaking to someone who was blocked
from her view by the angle of the chimney breast.

'Vera . . . Ian . . . let me introduce an old friend
of mine to you.' The thin, dark-haired woman
turned as Sue touched her arm, smiling charmingly at Kate and extending her hand. She had
that look of glossy perfection that Kate had come
to recognise as belonging to Londoners, but
despite the elegance of her appearance, the
immaculate make-up and the designer dress, the
smile she gave Kate was warm and genuinely
friendly.

'Sue's told us so much about you,' she told
Kate, 'and about your house. It sounds lovely.'

Her husband had turned away to talk to John,
but now he turned back, directing his attention
towards Kate, warm grey eyes twinkling slightly
as he took her extended hand. 'So *you* are Kate.'
He gave Sue a mock reproachful smile and

teased, 'Why didn't you tell me she was beautiful? I'd have left Vera at home.'

'No way,' his wife interrupted firmly, adding with a smile at Kate, 'Not that I imagine a girl like Kate would be interested in you anyway. I expect she has men queueing up to take her out.'

It wasn't the sort of teasing that Kate was used to, and she flushed a little, even while she realised there was no malice or unkindness in Vera's words, and was glad of Sue's timely interruption when she tapped her husband on the shoulder and asked him to get Kate a drink.

It was as John turned towards her that Kate had her first glimpse of the man he had been talking to, and in the same instant that her brain registered the familiarity of his features, hardened and honed by time though they were, her body froze. She couldn't move ... couldn't even breathe, could only stare at him like a petrified creature while distantly she was aware of Vera Benson chattering gaily, saying something that included both his name and her own. She saw him move ... reach out towards her, and a dreadful tearing panic took hold of her. She wanted to turn and flee, but as though she were trapped in some horrendous nightmare it was impossible for her to move.

'Kate...' The deep measured voice hadn't changed, nor the clipped curt way he said her name, even if he was saying it as though he had never heard it before, looking at her as though he had never set eyes on her before too.

Relief flooded through her, acting as a trigger to release her from her stunned paralysis.

He was extending his hand towards her, and she almost cringed away from touching it, but some deep instinct for protection urged her to take it, to behave as normally as she could.

He shook her hand, his fingers cool and hard against her own. Strange to think that she had once dreamed of those fingers against her skin . . . touching, caressing, bringing her to womanhood. She shuddered deeply and stepped back, completely unable to look into his face. Could it be that he hadn't recognised her? Oh, please God, let that be the case. She didn't think she could bear the humiliation of having to face him if he knew the truth.

'Dominic has just arrived from the States,' she heard Vera Benson explaining. 'He and my husband are in the same line of business— merchant banking.'

Merchant banking. Was that what he called it? Against her will, Kate felt a deep anger stir inside her. That weekend when Ricky brought Dominic Harland home with him, she hadn't realised why. That realisation had only come later after Ricky's death, when she discovered the extent of the money her late husband owed his old school-friend. It was Dominic who held a mortgage on the farmland surrounding the house and she had sold that land to repay his losses after Ricky died, but it wasn't because of that that she couldn't bear to face him.

'Come on, everyone, dinner's almost ready. Kate, you're next to Dominic,' Sue announced, shepherding them all towards the dining-room. Instinctively Kate stopped and looked across at him. He was staring back at her, the gold eyes darkly topaz, and as he watched her Kate knew that he had not forgotten ... that he *had* recognised her. Dark colour stained her normally pale skin as the agony of her memories convulsed her. Dear God, she had never thought she would ever see him again. She had prayed and hoped she would not, comforted in the worst moments of her self-torment by the knowledge that he was not a man who would ever reappear in her life, but now here he was, carrying with him information which could blast apart all that she had made of herself, and all that she had struggled to put aside after Ricky's death.

The meal was a nightmare, from which she surfaced briefly aware of the ebb and flow of comfortable conversation going on around her, but totally unable to take any part in it. She heard her name mentioned and looked up unguardedly, letting her glance mesh with Dominic Harland's. Anger and contempt burned in the gold depths of his eyes, scorching her.

'My goodness, how very interesting!'

She was aware of Vera Benson turning towards her with a warm smile, but felt totally unable to respond.

'You must come over and look at our conservatory,' the other woman was saying. 'It's been badly damaged, I'm afraid, and a lot of the glass needs replacing. I had been thinking in terms of something pretty and amusing in one of the panels.'

This was business, Kate told herself, struggling to break free of her own terror, forcing herself to respond and ask when it would be convenient for her to call.

'I'm not sure what our plans are at the moment—we're still based in London, but perhaps I could give you a ring, say, later in the week when I know what we're doing next weekend.'

Kate gave Vera her telephone number, making a mental note to mention to Harry that they would need business cards. She knew she ought to have been elated at the prospect of her first freelance commission, but she felt too weighed down with anxiety. Would Dominic Harland tell his friends what she had done? She closed her eyes. No . . . no, surely not . . .

'Kate! Kate, are you all right?'

She opened them again to be confronted by Sue's concerned face. 'You went quite white,' Sue explained worriedly. 'I thought for a moment you must be ill.'

Oh, if only she was. If only she could make that excuse and leave, but if she did Sue was bound to worry. It wasn't fair to her friend to disrupt her dinner party.

'Not ill . . . just slightly tired,' she fibbed. 'I stayed up too late last night . . .'

Out of the corner of her eye she saw Dominic's mouth curl downwards.

'It seems that widowhood hasn't changed your lifestyle then, Mrs Hammond.'

Kate wasn't sure who was the most shocked by his comment; Vera Benson was staring quite openly at him, while Sue's eyes had widened to their furthest extent. Neither of the other two couples seemed to have heard his remark, but John was looking at him, frowning slightly.

Please don't let me be sick, Kate prayed feverishly. Of them all, only she knew what Dominic meant.

'I was working,' she said tonelessly. 'An idea for a design——'

'I didn't realise you already knew Kate, Dominic,' Vera Benson interrupted, plainly puzzled that he had not mentioned it before.

'I knew her husband,' he corrected, his voice grating slightly as he looked across the table at Kate. 'He was—a client of mine.'

Suddenly it was almost too much for her. He was baiting her deliberately, she thought bitterly . . . he was deliberately trying to push her into . . . into what? Into admitting what she had once tried to do? But why? Oh, she could understand well enough why he might loathe and despise her, even why he should want to punish her . . . but didn't he realise he had already done that in the most effective way there was?

Suddenly too tired to pretend any longer, she looked directly at him, forcing herself to meet the cold blaze of his eyes.

'My late husband was a compulsive gambler,' she said wearily for Vera Benson's benefit, adding for Sue and John's, 'Mr Harland's company was the one that loaned Ricky money against the security of the farmland.'

'Very neat, Mrs Hammond, but I notice you were very careful not to explain exactly why your husband turned to gambling.'

His mouth was a tight line of anger, the bitter

words hitting her like bullets, making pain explode inside her. She had no defence against what he was saying. She wanted to cry out that it was not her fault she had not been the wife Ricky wanted, that it was not her fault that . . .

Instead she gathered all her self-control round her and speaking slowly and carefully, spacing out the words so that her voice wouldn't tremble, she said quietly, 'My friends don't require explanations, Mr Harland, and others don't warrant them.' Then she dropped her eyes to her plate and made a pretence of being totally involved in eating what was left of the chocolate mousse Sue had served.

She was also too aware of the atmosphere around her. Vera Benson was chatting animatedly to John, trying to pretend that nothing untoward had happened. Sue got up to remove their plates, and sensing a reprieve, Kate got up to help her.

Only when they were safely inside the kitchen did Sue speak, her fair skin flushing, anger darkening her soft blue eyes as she burst out, 'What an absolute rat! I swear, Kate, if I'd known, I'd never have agreed to have him here. The Bensons just asked if they could bring a friend.'

'Please, Sue, honestly it doesn't matter. You couldn't have known.'

'But he was so rude to you! What on earth was he trying to imply when he made that crack about your lifestyle?'

'I . . . I don't really know,' Kate lied. 'I only met him once when Ricky brought him home for a weekend. I've no idea what Ricky told him about the way we lived.'

'Not the truth, that's for sure,' Sue commented bluntly, 'otherwise he'd be singing a very different song. How on earth did Ricky come to be involved with him in the first place? Vera was telling me he's virtually a millionaire, very strait-laced and honourable in all his business dealings too, apparently—hardly Ricky's cup of tea, I would have thought.'

'No. He and Ricky were at school together, and Ricky's grandfather invited him to spend the holidays at the house a couple of times. His mother was South American, and his parents spent a lot of time over there. Ricky said something about his mother's family being extremely wealthy.'

'South American. Mmm . . . well, that would explain that fantastic tan . . . and those looks . . . Still, I think I'd rather have my John,' Sue commented. 'He might be a good-looker, but he's far too hard and judgmental for my taste. Of all the things to happen,' she wailed miserably, 'just when I'd persuaded you to come out of your shell a little!' She saw her friend's white face, and flung down the cloth she had picked up, grabbing Kate's arm instead. 'Oh, Kate, don't let him get to you,' she pleaded. 'It's obvious he doesn't know the first thing about you . . . the sort of person you are. He's obviously making his judgment of you on something Ricky must have told him, and we all know what Ricky was. Please don't let it upset you. If you like I'll get John to have a word with him and put him right.'

'No!' The sharp panicky denial sounded over-loud in the comfortable kitchen and Kate blenched again, saying more gently, 'No, honestly, Sue, it's okay. After all, I'm hardly likely to see him again, am I? It really doesn't matter what he thinks.' She forced a tight smile. 'Please ... let's just forget about the whole thing.'

'Okay, if that's what you want,' Sue agreed reluctantly. She had been looking forward to seeing Dominic Harland's arrogant face change when John told him the truth about poor Kate and about what Ricky had done to her.

'Come on, everyone will be waiting for their coffee,' Kate reminded her strategically.

Vera Benson came over to sit with Kate when Sue had served them their coffee in the drawing-room.

'I feel I must apologise for Dominic's be-haviour,' she said hesitantly to Kate. 'I honestly don't know what came over him. He's normally most charming. I hadn't even realised he knew you.'

There was a trace of speculation in her voice, and Kate said evenly, 'Well, we only met once when my husband brought him home for the weekend. Tell me, what exactly did you have in mind for this glass panel?' she asked, quickly changing the subject, but only listening with half her attention as her companion started to talk about her plans for the conservatory.

Kate wasn't the first to leave. The two couples who had travelled together went first, but once their car had disappeared, Kate, who had followed Sue and John into the hall, announced that she too must go. This way she could avoid having to say goodbye to Dominic Harland, and although Sue frowned a little, she let her go without too much protest.

For once her car started first time, but she was shaking so much that she crashed the gears badly as she took off down the drive. Not until she was home would she feel safe, if then. How could it have happened? How could fate have been unkind enough to thrust Dominic Harland back into the arena of her life, now, when she was finally making an attempt to get over the past?

# CHAPTER THREE

ONLY when she was safely back in her own home could she let the memories sweep over her, devastating her with their intensity, overwhelming her so much that she only had to close her eyes to be transported back to the past . . . To the morning after Dominic's arrival with Ricky.

She had been downstairs in the kitchen when Dominic walked into it, ducking to avoid the low beam close to the door.

As she turned to greet him that same flicker of sensation she had felt last night licked through her body, making her tense and stare up at him. He was taller than Ricky, and broader—much broader, she realised, the breath trapping in a spasm in her throat as she absorbed the masculinity of his torso beneath the thin material of his shirt. She wanted to look at him and go on looking at him, she realised feverishly, and more—she wanted to reach out and touch him, to . . .

'Ricky mentioned last night that you might be able to locate a spare razor for me . . . I forgot to bring mine.'

The cool censure in his voice snapped her back to reality, her nerve endings so raw that she practically flinched as he ran his hand raspingly against the stubble of his unshaven jaw.

It was an effort to drag her concentration away

from him, and force herself to remember where she had put Ricky's spare razor after she had had it mended.

By the time she had found it, she was trembling agitatedly, her confusion in no way leavened by his presence in the kitchen with her. It was a large enough room to hold a family, never mind two adults, and ordinarily it felt very spacious, but today for some reason the walls seemed to close claustrophobically around her, pressing in on her so that every time she moved she was intensely conscious of Dominic's presence.

He wasn't the first friend Ricky had brought home by any means, although lately Kate had grown used to not seeing her husband over the weekend—he normally stayed in London, where or who with she had no idea, nor any real wish to find out. Her marriage was a mockery of everything that marriage could be, but there was no way out of it for her. Ricky refused point-blank to even consider a divorce. Her mother, it seemed, was still giving him an annual allowance, which would naturally cease if they were divorced. 'And don't think she'll give you a home,' he had warned Kate the last time she had raised the subject of divorce, 'because she won't. She wants you even less than I do. God, when I think about it, what she's paying me to keep you out of her hair is peanuts!' His voice had turned ugly with malice and spite. 'And don't think anyone else would want you . . . what man in his right senses would want a cold bitch like you? Face it, Kate, it's either marriage to me or destitution, and since I'm not prepared to let you go, you don't really have a choice in any case.'

'Thanks.' The dry cool voice pierced through her thoughts, his fingertips cool and firm as they touched her hand briefly as he took the razor.

'I . . .'

He paused mid-stride towards the door and turned to look queryingly at her. Her heart was thumping heavily, a fine film of perspiration dampening her skin. What was she doing? Panic clawed wildly inside her as she recognised her own insane desire to keep him with her just a little longer.

'I'm just making Ricky a cup of tea. Would you like me to bring you one up as well?'

'Thanks.'

The door opened and he was gone. Kate leaned limply against the units, completely wrung-out emotionally and physically. What was happening to her? *You know what's happening*, a wry inner voice mocked. *You're a sex-starved wife who's suddenly found a man who can turn you on*.

She had got used to the sharply acid comments of this inner voice lately, and what it was saying to her now came uncomfortably close to the truth.

A surge of inner restlessness took over her, possessing her even though she tried to shake it off. Why shouldn't she be attracted to another man? After all, Ricky had no interest in her; he constantly humiliated her with his other women . . . She was twenty years old and, as far as she could see, condemned to a life of complete celibacy. Unless of course she took a lover . . .

Hard on the heels of this shocking thought

came the cynical knowledge that there must be more of her mother in her than she had ever thought. And yet why should it be so shocking for her to want to be made love to? She was a completely normally functioning female, wasn't she? She closed her eyes, trying to stem her turbulent, dangerous thoughts, but instead all she could see was Dominic Harland's dark, taut face, his hands reaching out to touch her body. Panting for breath she opened her eyes. This was ridiculous. But was it? Was it so unexpected that she should be attracted to him? Even with her inexperience she could see that very few women would be immune to such a man. The very cool hauteur with which he looked at her ignited a reckless need to see the coolness in his eyes change to hot passion. She wanted him, she acknowledged on a wave of very painful self-knowledge, she wanted him as mindlessly and needlessly as any female creature driven compulsively by an overriding inner urge to find a mate. But did he want her?

Telling herself that she was being a complete fool, she started to make the tea. How could a man like Dominic Harland want her when her own husband didn't? Strangely enough, the ache of Ricky's not wanting her, which she had long ago seemed to come to terms with, flared up anew, and refused to subside.

She made the tea and poured two cups, putting them on trays, and adding a couple of biscuits to each. She took Ricky's tray up first. Her husband was still deeply asleep, in the morning sunshine his face had an unhealthy pallor. Drained of the frenetic energy that seemed to possess him when he was awake, he looked almost lifeless.

Kate went downstairs for the other tray and carried it up to the guest suite, pausing to knock on the door outside. When there was no reply, she turned the handle and walked in.

She was just putting the tray down on the bedside table when the bathroom door opened. She turned automatically, colour seeping up under her skin as Dominic wandered into the bedroom, towelling his hair, the rest of his body completely nude.

Head bent, it was several seconds before he saw her. Seconds during which she could do nothing to alert him to her presence, seconds during which she simply stood and greedily and shamingly drank in the physical perfection of his body.

When he saw her, he didn't react at all as she had expected. Calmly wrapping the damp towel round his hips, he came towards her and said evenly, 'Tell me, Kate, how long have you and Rick been married?'

The question startled her, making her touch her tongue to suddenly dry lips and respond huskily in a cracked voice:

'Two years . . .'

'He must have married you almost out of the schoolroom.'

'I . . . Yes, I was eighteen . . .'

He was standing so close to her now that she could hardly breathe. He had showered and she could smell the fresh lemony scent of his soap on his skin, see the tiny beads of moisture slicking down the hair on his chest. Fine dark hair which, as she knew, ran in a narrow line over the hard flatness of his stomach, and then ... But no ... her body trembled as she tried to shut away the memory of how his naked body had looked.

Amazingly, suddenly he smiled at her, his eyes golden and amused as he said teasingly, 'I'm the one who should be embarrassed, you know, not you. After all, it isn't as though I was the first nude male you've ever seen, is it?'

When he smiled at her, really smiled properly, the creases alongside his mouth held just a suggestion of a dimple, and the look in his eyes seemed to bathe her in a golden heat.

Suddenly it all overwhelmed her, and she was embarrassed. Not by what she had seen, but that she had looked and gone on looking, and was even now feeling the thunderous reactions to the sight of him thudding through her veins. She turned to flee, an automatic, unthinking reaction, but he reacted just as automatically and far faster, blocking her exit, gripping her wrist and pulling her towards him, laughter glinting in his eyes as he shook his head.

'Running away?' He shook his head. 'You should never do that, you know.'

'Why not?' Kate asked the question without thinking, using the words to hold at bay her tumultuous reaction at being so close to him. She felt almost too weak to stand up, and had to fight to stop herself from swaying into his body.

'Because running away makes a man want to chase, and then do this.' His voice had dropped to a throaty whisper, as soothing and hypnotic as the purr of a jungle cat, but like the jungle cat he was most dangerous when he seemed to be most gentle, and Kate gasped her shock, as her girlish daydreams were suddenly transformed into reality, and his grip on her tightened, his head bending so that his mouth could taste hers.

Ricky had kissed her before they were married, but never like this, never using his tongue to tease and prise apart the softness of her lips; never in a way that made all her insides melt and then burn liquid pleasure so that she wanted the kiss to go on and on.

When his mouth left hers, Kate could only stare up at him in bemused delight, her mouth slightly parted, innocently begging for more, but the humour had gone from his eyes, and now they glowed dark amber. Even her innocence could not protect her from the anger and contempt she could see bracketing his mouth, and a terrible sense of somehow having disappointed him flooded through her. She disengaged herself from his embrace and stepped back, unaware of the damp patches on her blouse where she had been pressed against him, too conscious of the intense constraint in the air around them to consider anything else.

Dominic didn't look at her as she fled for the door, simply standing with his back to her and his head slightly bowed.

*Why* had he kissed her? It was a question she asked herself ceaselessly through the day. Ricky had taken Dominic out, ostensibly to look round the estate, and she had been surprised to learn that Dominic had spent the odd holiday at the house during his schooldays.

'Your grandfather was a very rare man,' he had commented to Ricky over the late breakfast she had prepared for them. 'You were lucky to have him, Rick.'

Her husband had just shrugged, and Kate, who well knew her husband's view of the gentle old man who had brought him up, wondered if Dominic knew her husband as well as he thought. Ricky had despised his grandfather, and had been contemptuous and bitter of all the money he had given to local charities, claiming that charity began at home, and that he had far more need of it.

It was while she was preparing the evening meal that an answer to the question that had been tormenting her all day presented itself to her.

Dominic was a very experienced and worldly man, no doubt he had had even more affairs than Ricky. No doubt he had kissed her simply in automatic reaction to her presence. A tiny thrill of pain sliced through her, quickly followed by the heady knowledge that he must have wanted to kiss her. And if he had wanted to kiss her, might he also not want to make love to her?

She wanted him as her lover, Kate knew that now. She also knew that she ought to feel ashamed of herself for doing so, but the tensions created by her marriage had coalesced into a violent need to prove that she was womanly and desirable.

Her preparations for the evening meal finished, she wandered into the drawing-room and picked up the book she had been reading the previous evening. It was an historical saga set during the Wars of the Roses, and the heroine, who was in love with a man fighting on the other side to that favoured by her family, had been caught near the castle of this man and taken to him. He had accused her of being a spy, and she had been forced to admit to him that she had been watching the castle purely to get a glimpse of him, because she loved him. He had not believed her, and now she was sitting in the chamber he had given her while he decided what to do with her, trying desperately to find a way to prove to him the truth of her words.

Kate read on, not really interested in the book, her mind racing ahead to when the men returned, until something caught her eye and then she read feverishly, devouring the printed page and then going back to read it again. She put the book down face-open on the floor and closed her eyes, knowing she had just found the solution to her own dilemma. Heavens, it must have been Fate that had made her pick that particular book from the library. But could she carry it off . . . could she do what the heroine had done? Could she go up to Dominic's room tonight and get into his bed, to wait for him there?

As a plan it was hardly practical, she told herself. What about Ricky?

Unwillingly she abandoned the idea, her body aching with disappointment. She so longed for Dominic to make love to her, and if that was wrong, well then, it was wrong. Wasn't it just as wrong for Ricky to marry her and keep her as a wife who was no real wife?

It was late when the two men returned, and she could smell drink on Ricky's breath.

However, it was Dominic who apologised, and not her husband, but Kate was so used to his unreliability that she had deliberately not started the evening meal.

Sensing Rick's mood, she made an excuse of having eaten alone earlier to get her out of sitting down with them. When he was like this Ricky could snipe cruelly at her, and she felt far too fragile tonight to cope with his sarcasm.

Half an hour after she had taken them their coffee, Ricky came into the kitchen and announced belligerently, 'I'm going out . . . I'm sick to death of this place!'

'Out . . . but what about Dominic?'

'Dominic?' His lip curled and if she hadn't known better, Kate might almost have thought he actively disliked the man he had called his friend. 'He's in the study reading the diaries.'

The diaries had been written by Ricky's grandfather and great-grandfather. Kate had read them herself and had found them fascinating, but Ricky considered them 'boring'.

'Where . . . where are you going?'

'What the hell has that got to do with you?' Ricky snarled, adding as he pushed open the back door, 'And don't bother waiting up for me . . . I might not bother coming back—at least not tonight.'

It was no worse than anything he had done before, but even so, Kate felt an aching coil of anger spring to life inside her. Only the knowledge that Ricky was all too likely to react physically and violently to any criticism she might make kept her silent.

She waited for half an hour and then went into the study. Dominic was seated behind the desk, engrossed in what he was reading. She cleared her throat and he looked up frowning slightly, his frown clearing as he saw her.

'I just came to ask if you would like more coffee. Ricky's gone out, by the way . . .'

Her voice died away as he frowned and glanced at his watch. 'No coffee, thanks,' he told her. 'It's almost eleven and I think I'll have an early night. All that fresh air today tired me out—I'm not used to it. That's what living in London does for one. I'll just finish this chapter and then I'll go up.'

It was only as she closed the study door that Kate realised with heart-thumping intensity what she intended to do. Quickly, before she could lose her courage, she raced upstairs.

Fifteen minutes later she was lying self-consciously in the middle of the guest room bed, waiting for Dominic to arrive.

He saw her the moment he stepped into the room, his body freezing as he snapped on the light and it illuminated her presence in his bed.

Fear and excitement mingled, making her heart leap and the blood soar through her veins as she saw the way his face changed, male desire dominating every feature, making her tremble with weakness. But even as her brain recognised that she had achieved her objective and her body reacted nervously to that recognition, his face changed, hardening, darkening, until there was nothing but contempt and anger to be read in the bitter darkness of his eyes.

Advancing towards the bed, he paused at the foot of it, to stare at her with cold eyes and a hard mouth. For what seemed like an eternity he simply studied her, his icy scrutiny making her go cold with shame and humiliation. How could she have thought she saw desire in his eyes? She had plainly deluded herself. Now, when it was far too late, she bitterly regretted the impulse that had brought her here to his room . . . to his bed.

'Just what the hell do you think you're doing?'

The harsh words cut into her like thin whips, destroying what was left of her composure.

She desperately wanted to cry, to close her eyes and open them again to discover this was all a nightmare, but some part of her stubbornly refused to allow her to avoid the consequences of her actions. She had been so desperate to prove to herself that she was feminine and desirable that she had made no allowances for this scenario, and had no idea of how to cope with it.

Instead all she could do was stammer painfully, 'I wanted . . .'

'I know quite well what you wanted,' Dominic cut her off, his mouth twisting as he added coldly, 'but you're not going to get it . . . at least not tonight, and most definitely not from me.'

As he spoke he came towards her, wrenching back the bedclothes and dragging her out of his bed. She averted her eyes from his in shamed distress, her teeth clenching together as she caught his sharply indrawn breath, and felt his fingers bite even more painfully into her arm.

His touch hurt and she whimpered deep in her throat, intimidated by an anger and contempt that seemed to reinforce all the unkind gibes Ricky had thrown at her, and which for some reason seemed to hurt far, far more. As she instinctively arched away from the contact of his flesh against her own, she heard Dominic curse, and then say harshly, 'It's too late to play the injured innocent now. My God,' he added thickly, 'does Rick know what kind of wanton he's married? No wonder he drinks and gambles so heavily!'

Kate wanted to protest that he was wrong ... but her throat ached too badly, her muscles bunched in agonised protest at the way he had destroyed all her hopes and illusions. She wanted him to go away and leave her alone so that she could go back to her own room and hide herself away, as much from her own inner sense of humiliation as from him, but he didn't seem disposed to do any such thing.

Swallowing down the painful lump in her throat, she whispered achingly, 'Please ...' stopping abruptly as she caught the savagery of his indrawn breath and felt the anger tremor through him as his eyes glittered darkly into her own.

'You ask *me* for pity?' he demanded softly. 'It's Rick who gets that. *This* is what you deserve.'

He bent over her, his body blocking out most of the light, fear keeping her body rigid as his mouth ground down on hers. She could taste whisky on his breath; feel the tension and rage in his body as his mouth savaged hers, in a kiss that was a parody of all that a kiss should be.

She felt her inner lip split beneath the pressure

of his mouth, and tasted the rusty iron flavour of her own blood. She was under no illusion about what he was doing, and when at last he released her mouth she told herself that she was lucky that previously all she had suffered from her husband had been his indifference. Perhaps she ought to be grateful to Dominic, she thought miserably, forcing down the weak tears building up her eyes, because now she knew just how lucky she was that she had not been forced to endure Ricky's hatred.

Numbly she was aware of him picking her up, and striding towards the door. Terror held her silent as he thrust open her own bedroom door and carried her to the bed, dropping her callously down on to it.

She forced herself to keep her eyes open and her body still until she was sure he had gone, and even then she couldn't relax. Terror held her completely immobile.

She wasn't sure how long it was before she was able to get up and stumble into her bathroom. She felt abused, degraded in the worst possible way, more contaminated somehow than if he had been a stranger who had callously attacked and raped her, because then at least she would have been free of the taint of having invited what had happened.

It was only a kiss, she told herself feverishly as she scrubbed at her pale skin . . . a kiss, that was all, but inside she felt so scarred and mutilated that she didn't think she would ever be the same again. But the fault was hers . . . she had been the one who was to blame . . . And yet she couldn't help thinking that had she been one of the beauties Ricky openly dated, he would not have reacted to her in the same way ... no, it was something in her that had caused him to reject and humiliate her ... something in her that was lacking, that made it impossible for any man to feel anything other than disgust for her. At last, exhausted by the trauma of the evening and completely drained of energy, she climbed into bed.

Tonight something inside her had died and she didn't think it could ever be brought back to life again. From now on she would live her life as though she were a nun. No man would ever get the chance to do to her what first Ricky, and then Dominic, had done.

The harsh ring of the telephone jerked her abruptly from the past to the present. Numbly Kate reached for the receiver.

'Kate?'

Sue's familiar voice sounded faintly anxious.

'I was just ringing to check that you got back all right—and to apologise again for what happened.'

Soothing her friend's apprehensions helped her to close her mind on the past, although she could feel the tension flaring inside her when Sue added, 'I had no idea you and he had met before, or that he was a friend of Rick's.'

'Sue, I've got some milk on for a cup of chocolate, I'd better go before it boils over.'

It was a lie, but it got her out of answering any more questions. Damn Dominic Harland, Kate thought bitterly as she replaced the receiver. What malign whim of the gods had brought him back into her life just when a clear new future seemed to promise freedom from the pain of the past?

# CHAPTER FOUR

IT was lunchtime the following day before Kate felt as though she was beginning to get Dominic Harland's unwanted presence on the fringes of her mind, back into proper perspective, and that alone was disturbing.

She had promised herself, once she had managed to drag herself free of the morass of self-loathing and misery that had drained her of the willpower to do anything other than merely exist from day to day for months after that dreadful weekend, that henceforward she was not going to waste a single second's thought on Dominic, or what he might think of her.

That he had made totally incorrect assumptions about her morality she knew very well, but logic—something she had developed within herself with fierce zeal after her meeting with him—had imposed upon her that no matter how much she might differ from the type of woman he had obviously thought her to be, her motives on that particular night were not open to any kind of misinterpretation. She had quite simply wanted him to make love to her so that in doing so she could shed the misery of knowing herself unwanted by Ricky.

Another woman, she knew, might have developed a fierce hatred of Dominic for his rejection of her, but in her, that hatred had been turned in upon herself, burning away what she now chose to think of as her stupidity and weakness in convincing herself that she could find the answer to her own inadequacies in a man's arms. Now all that was past. She no longer allowed herself to even think of men in any sexual sense. It was safer that way ... much, much safer. Never again was she going to allow herself to be as vulnerable to pain and humiliation as she had been with Dominic.

Midway through the afternoon an unanticipated telephone call from Vera disrupted her hard-won calm.

The other woman was telephoning to suggest a time for them to meet to discuss her conservatory. Her voice sounded slightly strained, and Kate guessed intuitively that Vera felt uncomfortable about what had happened at the dinner party. Her initial instinct to cut herself off from the hazard of any potential contact with Dominic, no matter how slightly, was overridden by stubborn pride, as an inner voice taunted her that if she refused to meet Vera now, and Dominic got to hear of it, he would assume that she was afraid. So when Vera suggested that she call round at the house the following day at two-thirty, Kate found herself agreeing.

It was irritating that this should happen now, just when she had felt that life was starting to blossom out a little for her. Would Dominic's opinion of her affect her chances of getting a commission from the Bensons?

Why should it? she asked herself hardily. Vera would judge her on her ideas and abilities, surely

not on her supposed morals or lack of them. Even
so it was unpleasant and disconcerting to think
that Dominic might have discussed her with
them in a derogatory fashion. Her mouth
hardened slightly. She was not going to be
pushed into a position where she had to defend
herself against some supposed crime. If pressed
by either Dominic himself or anyone else, she
would simply . . . What? Tell the truth and shame
the devil? The aptness of the old saying made her
mouth twist in wry self-mockery. What she had
done was not really so very dreadful—logic told
her that, but logic could not wipe away the agony
of Dominic's harsh condemnation and rejection,
and it was that that had left scars that hurt and
tormented her even now.

More to keep her mind occupied than anything
else, she drove into the small local market town,
intent on visiting the library and getting out
whatever books she could on Victorian archi-
tecture. The conservatory had come to full power
during Victorian times and by studying the
period in more depth she might come up with
some ideas that could be incorporated into a
design for Vera's conservatory.

While she was in town she paid a visit to the
office of an estate agent, mindful of the fact that
it was time she got the house on the market for
sale.

The partner she spoke to was somewhere in his
early thirties, his manner pleasant, with what she
suspected was supposed to be a flattering edge of
flirtatiousness. This she ignored, her smile
frostily cool, as she refused to respond. No doubt

he used the same manner on all his female clients,
and it was rather an insult to her intelligence that
he should suppose she could believe that he
might be genuine. After all, she knew exactly
how little appeal she had for the male sex, didn't
she?

'I'll come out and look at the house later in the
week, if I may?' he suggested, when he had
finished taking down the details. 'When would
suit you?'

It was left that Kate would ring him later in the
week when she knew what her movements would
be. In many ways she should not be entirely sorry
to sell up and move. The house had far too many
unhappy memories for her. Perhaps once she was
installed in the cottage . . . But there could be no
going back, she reminded herself as she stepped
out into the sunshine. She could not be again the
girl she had been at seventeen.

On impulse on the way back home she made a
detour so that she could stop at the cottage. It
had a deserted, faintly forlorn air, the garden
untidily overgrown. Since she had not brought
the keys she could not go inside, but she was
pleased to see that the sturdily built stone cottage
had all its roof slates in place and that the gutters
and drainpipes were all in good condition.

She had been happy here in this snug,
protective house, and she would be happy here
again, she told herself stoutly, blinking away the
lump of emotion rising in her throat. Her
marriage to Ricky had come so quickly after her
father's death that she had never felt she had
truly been given time to mourn her parent. In

fact now, as an adult, she could see that she had gone into her marriage in a complete state of shock, but she was not going to start blaming others for what had happened in the past; she had believed herself in love with Ricky. She and her mother had never been close, and she suspected that even if the latter had offered her a home in America with her, she would not have been happy there.

The clouds which had merely been a faint shadow on the horizon when she set out suddenly obliterated the sun. Shivering in the thinness of her T-shirt and skirt, Kate looked up at them and saw that they held the threat of rain. It was time she was going anyway.

She reached home just as the first large raindrops hit her windscreen, and climbed out of the car, making a quick dash for the door, her library books clutched under her arm.

Now that she had made the decision to put the house on the market she looked at it with new eyes. The hall was large and welcoming, the galleried landing drawing the eye. It was the sort of house that would appeal most to people like the Bensons; newcomers to the area with enough money to buy and maintain such an expensive property.

Up until quite recently, Kate had done all the housework herself, and she still did the majority of it, although now she employed someone to come out from the village twice a week, to help out.

She made herself a cup of coffee and took it into the library with her. Here was where she worked. She found the comfortable, masculine ambience of the book-filled room relaxing. She kept her portfolio of designs in a drawer of the large partner's desk set across one corner of the room, and as she reached for it, she switched on the desk lamp.

The rain clouds covered the sky now, and the small lead-paned windows let in precious little light at the best of times.

As she sat down and started to look through her portfolio a mental image of Dominic's face intruded between her concentration and the delicate drawings on the white sheets. It irritated her that he should have this power to come between her and her work. She should have been feeling elated and excited at the prospect of a new commission, but all she could feel was an overwrought tension that made her too jumpy and nervous to concentrate on anything.

She reached for the telephone and dialled Harry's number. Liz answered the phone, her cheerful, warm tones helping to banish the tense mood which had enveloped her. They chatted for several minutes while Liz sent someone to fetch her husband from his workshop.

'I'm really glad that you're going to go into partnership with Harry, love,' Liz told her. 'It's given him a new lease on life . . . He's as excited about it as a little boy.' She gave a rich chuckle and added. 'He can't stop talking about it for two minutes together! Oh, here he is now,' she told Kate, relinquishing the receiver to her husband.

Briefly Kate told Harry about her meeting with Vera, and the other's interest in her work, adding that she had an appointment to see Vera the next day.

Harry was as enthusiastic as she had known he would be, banishing her self-doubts with his praise of her work and ideas, restoring some of the self-confidence in herself which seeing Dominic had destroyed.

'Don't make the mistake of going for something too heavy and stylised,' Harry warned her. 'It's surprising how well the modern free-form designs go with these traditional conservatories. Remember that one I showed you with the climbing roses?'

'Yes, I do. I must admit I was thinking of something along those lines, but quite what, I'm not sure yet.'

'Mmm . . . or there's always the alternative of a picture window. I saw a fantastic one the other day, where was it now . . .?'

As always when she was listening to Harry, Kate found her tense muscles relaxing as she allowed herself to be drawn into the magic of their shared interest. By the time she replaced the receiver her mind was seething with ideas.

Reaching for a piece of paper, she began to sketch quickly, and then more slowly as she became absorbed in what she was doing.

The dam of creativity that seeing Dominic had sealed in her mind, once broken, seemed to unleash a positive torrent of inspiration, and it was gone nine o'clock when she finally lifted her head, flexing tired fingers as she put down her pencil.

The late afternoon and evening had gone

without her even being aware of it, and now she felt both tired and slightly hungry, but it was a good tiredness; not the exhaustion of misery and hopelessness that she knew so well from the past.

Tidying up her papers and putting them in a folder, she went into the kitchen to make herself a cup of coffee and a light chicken salad supper which she took back to the library with her, this time curling up into the deep leather chair beside the fire with one of the books she had got from the library on her knee.

It was gone eleven when she finally went upstairs, her mind relaxed, warmed by the knowledge that the work she had done this evening was good.

Perhaps it was because she was feeling so relaxed and off her guard that she allowed herself to give in to the malign impulse that took her not to her own bedroom door, but to the door of the guest suite, which she pushed open.

From the doorway she could see the bed with its immaculate duvet and pillows.

After Ricky's death on an impulsive whim she had thrown out all the bedding from this room and replaced it. Her mouth twisted with wry self-mockery as she wondered what had made her replace the previous gold and brown colour scheme with a completely fresh one in pale lemons, greys and white. Her glance lingered on the traditional mahogany bed with its head and footboards. There was no doubt that the crisply laundered white cotton and linen duvet and pillows set off the room's delicate colour scheme, but had there been some deeper mental reason for her choosing white, the colour of purity, for the bedding in this particular room?

All at once her pleasantly relaxed mood was gone, the tension she had experienced earlier returning with full force. She wasn't going to think about Dominic, she told herself sternly as she closed the door and made her way to her own room. She had tortured herself enough over the past as it was; made herself pay a penance in lost self-respect that still left scars, but it was over now.

The house had five bedrooms, and the one that she now used had once been the nursery. She had moved into it immediately after Ricky's death, unable to bear the thought of going back to the room where he had taught her how undesirable he had found her as a woman. Had there again been some subtle motive in her picking this room out of them all? she wondered cynically as she started to undress. Had she chosen it knowing that as long as she owned the house, there would never be any need for nurseries?

As she turned into the drive leading to The Grange, Kate expelled a faint sigh of relief. Her little car had been more than usually reluctant to start this morning and in fact, on more than one occasion on the way here, the engine note had wavered ominously as though about to cut out. She would have to call at the garage on the way back, she decided, admitting to herself that it was high time she changed her car. Perhaps once she had sold the house there might be enough money to spare for her to do that.

Certainly she needed a reliable vehicle now that she was working.

Signs of the Bensons' occupation were already present in the gardens where Kate could see a local contract gardening firm at work on the overgrown lawns and flower beds.

The Grange was one of the darkly pebble-dashed ugly square houses of which the Victorians had seemed inordinately fond, as though their sheer size and bulk was impressive enough without any considerations needing to be made to artistic design. Kate had been inside on a couple of occasions before many years ago when her father had been alive, but the musty, dusty smell of disuse which she associated with the house was no longer in evidence when Vera opened the front door to her knock.

Instead she could smell new paint, her eyes widening admiringly over what she remembered as a darkly gloomy hall, which Vera had transformed completely.

'Vera, this is lovely!' Kate exclaimed enthusiastically, formality forgotten as she went closer to examine the newly rag-rolled walls. Two shades of the same colours had been used; a soft bluey green, ragged with pale gold; the lighter colours used above the dado rail and the darker below. She looked upwards and saw that the ceiling had been flat-painted in the darker bluey green, the cornice picked out in white.

'I'm glad you like it.' Vera's face lit up and she grinned conspiratorially at Kate. 'Ian thought it might be a bit over the top.' She gestured towards the staircase and added wryly, 'This monstrosity was put in just after the First World War, and I've decided to have it marbled, along with the dado rail—what do you think?'

'I think it will look stunning,' Kate told her honestly. 'And after all, ragging and marbling, and in fact all these finishes they're using nowadays, are very traditional arts, so it won't be at all out of keeping.'

'Mmm, that's what I thought. Come on into the drawing-room. We haven't touched it yet, but it's the only place where there's any furniture.'

Kate hadn't been in the drawing-room on her previous visits and she discovered that it was a well proportioned room with two of the deep bay windows the Victorians were so fond of, both overlooking the rear gardens, while two smaller windows on the fireplace wall overlooked the wide lawns.

The room looked as though it hadn't been touched in years. The walls were a filthy grey-cream, the carpet threadbare.

'The estate agent explained to us that the Colonel lived here on his own for over twenty years before he died,' Vera commented to Kate. 'And then the house was empty for three years.'

'Mmm . . . his nephew was asking an exorbitant price for it. The rumour was locally that the Colonel had stipulated that the property was not to be sold for development, but that his nephew was holding out for a high price, hoping in the end that it would remain empty for so long that it would have to be sold for the land. The gardens are quite extensive, aren't they?'

'Almost four acres, and with the number of

people now ready to commute this far to London, any houses built on it could have commanded a very good price. It's going to take years to get it the way we want it, but it will be worthwhile in the end. The children will love it.'

Vera saw Kate's surprise and smiled again. 'They're both at boarding school, I'm afraid. One of the reasons we've moved out here is that it will be much easier for them to go to day school.' She mentioned the name of a very famous school, and added, 'They take pupils as non-boarders. Ian and I were both boarders, and we both hated it.' Vera paused and added diffidently, 'As a matter of fact, Ian and Dominic were at school together, which must have meant that Ian knew your husband, although of course Ian is four years older than Dominic, and your husband, I believe, was younger?'

'Yes.'

Kate could feel the tension creeping through her body. She didn't want to talk about the past, about anything to do with Dominic Harland, but Vera seemed to be oblivious to her reluctance to pursue the subject, for she continued slowly, 'Poor Dominic, he had a most tragic childhood. His mother left his father for another man. Dominic was only two at the time, and after that he only saw his mother on a handful of occasions.

'His father was very bitter, he never let Dominic forget what his mother had done. In fact he brought him up to think of all women as treacherous and devious, and sending him to an all-boys school didn't help.'

Stonily Kate refused to comment or sympathise. If she had heard the story about anyone other than Dominic she knew she would have felt an instant empathy towards them, a sense of fellow feeling, but she would not allow herself to feel like that towards Dominic.

'I'm sorry you and Dominic seemed to get off on the wrong foot the other night,' Vera continued quietly. 'I've honestly never seen him behave quite like that before. Oh, he's always been very cool and wary if a woman comes on to him strongly, but . . .'

'Please could we change the subject?' Kate offered her hostess a wry smile to palliate the curt effect of her request. 'What happened in the past is past as far as I'm concerned,' she added, striving for a more relaxed note. 'Ricky's been dead for almost six years, and whatever our differences were, they're now over and done with. I can't criticise a man who's no longer alive to defend himself. All I will say is that I never encouraged or incited Ricky to gamble.'

Vera looked quite horrified, reaching over to cover one of Kate's hands with her own.

'Oh, my dear, no . . . I never thought for a moment that you had,' she exclaimed in a shocked voice. 'As I said, my husband doesn't remember Rick from school, but he is aware of who he was and how he lived . . .' She frowned slightly and added, 'As far as Dominic is concerned . . .'

Kate had heard enough. Already her stomach was knotted with pain and anxiety. 'Please,' she begged, 'may we just drop the whole subject? I . . .' To her consternation tears blurred her eyes. She blinked quickly, but not before her hostess had seen them. As she lowered her head defensively, Kate was dimly conscious of her hostess looking over her shoulder, but the reason for the arrested expression on Vera's face was lost on her until she heard her exclaiming, faintly apprehensively, 'Oh, Dominic, there you are! I thought you'd gone out . . .'

As she grappled with the implications of Vera's greeting, Kate was just glad that she had her back to the door. She would have hated him to see her like this, weak and tearful . . . vulnerable . . .

For heaven's sake, she chided herself, sitting up straighter and refusing to look around. What was the matter with her? Dominic could not hurt her now. So once she had believed herself attracted to him; had thought she had seen in him all the compassion and security lacking in her husband, and she had been wrong. So once he had spurned her, humiliating and hurting her badly, but that was all in the past, she told herself firmly, her back stiffening slightly as a sixth sense told her that he was getting closer to them.

'Dominic is staying with us for a while,' she told Kate brightly. 'He and my husband . . .'

'I'm sure that Mrs Hammond isn't interested in my reasons for being down here, Vera.'

Kate wasn't surprised to see the older woman colour slightly under the cool hauteur of Dominic's voice, and, angry on Vera's behalf, she turned sharply to face him, catching her breath as she realised how far back she had to tilt her head to look into his face, her voice as cool as his had been as she said, 'You're quite right. I'm not the least bit interested.'

The distantly polite smile she gave him was all that saved the words from being downright rude, but she was beyond caring about that now, and turning her back on him she said calmly to Vera, 'Perhaps it isn't convenient for me to discuss the conservatory with you now. I'll . . .' She made to get up, but Vera protested quickly,

'Oh no . . . of course it is.' She got up. 'Please come through and have a look at it.'

In order to follow her, Kate would have had to brush past Dominic, almost touching him, but instead, she made a deliberate detour, not even looking at him as she followed her hostess's hurried footsteps.

The conservatory was attached to the opposite side of the house, very traditional in design, with a typical, high vaulted roof, the glass panels supported by delicate wrought iron work.

'I've had the gardening contractors clean everything out,' Vera told Kate as they stepped on to the marble tiled floor. She wrinkled her nose slightly. 'It looks awful at the moment, but . . .'

'But the potential's there,' Kate finished for her with a smile, banishing from her mind her mental image of Dominic's darkly brooding features as she forced herself to concentrate on the conservatory.

She had brought her portfolio with her, and sitting down on a wrought iron bench she opened it to show Vera.

Half an hour later Vera said enthusiastically, 'Kate, they're all lovely, but I think you know

I've fallen for the freestyle design of the cottage garden flowers.'

Kate knew the one she meant; a rather over-the-top design which would cover all three sides of the conservatory with the glowing colours of traditional cottage garden plants.

'It will be expensive,' she warned Vera now.

'Mmm ... I can see that, but could you leave the sketch with me to show Ian?' Vera made a slight face and added wryly, 'In his business he has to do a certain amount of entertaining—the kind where it's important to create a good impression. It's not really my style, but it is something I have to do. Your design for the conservatory would make a stunning visual impact—you know how it is, there's a certain amount of vying for supremacy among that sort of set, and I suspect our American visitors will be particularly impressed, but I do want Ian to see it before I commit myself.'

'I quite understand that,' Kate assured her, her brain ringing with the implications of what Vera was saying. The sketch she had favoured had been one Kate had only done on a last-minute impulse, loving the idea of it, but knowing that very few people would be able to afford such extravagance. It had never occurred to her that Vera Benson might actually opt for it. It just went to show how much money there was in merchant banking, Kate thought wryly, collecting her sketches together. The cost of implementing her design into the conservatory would probably have enabled her to run the house for another three or four years, but then she was not in the

Bensons' income bracket, nor had ever wanted to be, she acknowledged.

Now that the first shock of hearing Vera say she liked the design had passed, she was beginning to realise what a challenge implementing it would be, and what a marvellous opportunity for Harry and herself as one of their first ventures in their new partnership.

All of a sudden she couldn't wait to get home and tell him all about it.

There was no sign of Dominic as Vera showed her to the front door, and imperceptibly the tension that had gripped her as they left the conservatory eased. Having thanked Vera and made her farewells Kate got into her car. Vera stood in the open doorway, frowning slightly as she witnessed Kate's unsuccessful attempts to get the recalcitrant vehicle started.

It wasn't going to start, Kate recognised balefully after ten fruitless minutes trying to get a response, and what was more, with each attempt the battery was getting flatter and flatter.

At last she was forced to recognise defeat, and getting out of the car, she asked Vera if she might use her phone.

'Of course ... I'd run you home myself, but I'm afraid Ian's got the car.'

Kate was just about to follow Vera back into the house when Dominic walked round the side of it, frowning as he saw Kate's car and the two women.

'What's wrong?' he asked crisply, his question directed at Vera, not at herself, Kate recognised. In some strange way it was almost as though

Dominic himself considered his outburst on the evening of the dinner party as some sort of mental aberration, to judge by the way he was now studiously ignoring her.

'Kate's car won't start,' Vera told him worriedly, 'and I can't offer her a lift because I don't have my car . . .'

Before she could say anything else Kate interrupted quickly, 'That wouldn't have been necessary in any case, thanks, Vera. I can get the garage to pick me up and drop me at Sue's. She'll give me a lift home.'

Quite by chance she caught a glimpse of Dominic's face as he registered her remarks. The scorn and contempt in his eyes was almost like a physical blow. It hurt so much that the intensity of the pain froze her as she waited like a trapped animal for it to subside. What was wrong with her? Why should anything this man said either to her or about her have the power to hurt now? Once she had acted irrationally and stupidly and she had paid for that mistake . . . Oh, how she had paid . . . but she *had* paid.

'There's no need to do any of that,' he announced laconically, his eyes on Kate's face, but his words directed to Vera, as he added, 'I can give Mrs Hammond a lift home. I was just about to go into the village anyway . . . I assume that's where the garage is,' he asked Kate, continuing before she could confirm or deny his remark. 'We can call there on the way and get them to come out to your car . . . What's wrong with it, by the way?'

He walked over to her ancient Mini and stood

looking at it. He still moved with that same
indolent masculinity that had had such an effect
on her eight years ago, Kate acknowledged, but
now she was not an impressionable twenty-year-
old. So why was her stomach doing crazy,
physically impossible stunts?

Not because she was attracted to him. No, it
was more likely to be fear that was making her
tummy loop the loop and then clench into tight
knots.

'It won't start,' she told him distractedly,
dragging her gaze away from the amber scrutiny
of his as he paused and then reached inside her
car to release the bonnet mechanism.

She saw him frown as he looked inside, and it
struck her that he might have thought that she
was manufacturing her car's ailment, although for
what purpose . . . A slow burn of colour spread
through her body as she realised he might think
she was deliberately engineering a situation
which would throw them together, but no . . .
how could she have known that Vera had no car
. . . or for that matter that he would appear just at
the crucial moment. She was letting her imagination run away with her, she chided herself, but
she still found herself letting her breath out in a
silent easing of tension when he lifted his head
from the engine inside the bonnet and said dryly,
'The starter-motor seems to have packed in, and
there seem to be several electrical faults as well.'
As he closed the bonnet and stood up he
addressed Kate directly for the first time, saying
mockingly, 'Why on earth don't you buy yourself
a newer model?'

His very obvious contempt for her, his air of self-assurance, and the distinctly unpleasant manner in which he had treated her coalesced into a seething mass of resentment that caused her fingers to curl tightly into her palms, her voice curt and hostile as she snapped back, 'Quite simply because I can't afford to.' Facing him directly, she added bitingly, 'And please don't worry about giving me a lift. If Vera would allow me to use her telephone . . .'

Behind her she heard the faint sound of distress made by her hostess. So she was being rude, so what? Kate thought on a sudden surge of adrenalin-induced feeling of bravery. She was not going to be browbeaten by anyone, least of all by Dominic Harland.

'I'm not worried about it.' The sudden sensation of his fingers closing round her upper arm caused Kate to whirl round in acute disbelief. It seemed incredible to her that he should actually touch her, and her eyes unknowingly betrayed that disbelief to him.

It was extremly disconcerting to see the run of dark colour spread under his skin, as his eyes shifted away from her own, his hand dropping away from her. Instinctively she stepped back, breathing deeply as though somehow having him so close to her had robbed the atmosphere of oxygen.

'Get in the car,' he told her quietly.

Suddenly she was too drained to argue, and what was she protesting about anyway? She could see Vera watching them curiously. The last thing she wanted to do was to promote any gossip

about the past. There would be those in the
village who would remember his visit all those
years ago, and who could put two and two
together and easily make five. The village thrived
on gossip, and she had no wish to be the subject
of it. There had been enough during the days
when Ricky was still alive.

Dominic's car was parked to one side of her
own, a gold BMW that looked brand new, which
she supposed it must be if he had only just come
to this country from America.

The passenger door was unlocked and as she got
inside she dismissed the idea that it might only be
hired, and marvelled a little about the differences
between the lifestyle of people like the Bensons
and Dominic and herself. Unless of course he was
planning to move back to England?

Telling herself that it was really of no interest
to her what he did, she tensed instinctively as he
got into the car beside her. Vera came to wave
them off, shielding her eyes from the afternoon
sun.

The car was smooth and powerful. Strapped
into her seat, Kate concentrated on looking out of
the window, not once allowing her glance to be
drawn to the man seated beside her.

She had nothing to say to him that could be
said without her betraying her agony over the
past, and she was glad that he too kept silent.

As they drove into the village and a group of
the locals outside the post office broke off their
conversation to admire the car, it struck her for
the first time that with the Bensons living
locally, Dominic might become more of a

permanent fixture in the area than she had first supposed. The thought was distinctly unpalatable, causing her to blench slightly and curl protesting fingers into her palms.

At the garage Dominic took charge, explaining quickly and explicitly about her car. Resentment raged inside Kate as she listened to him. She was used to running her own life—taking charge of her own affairs—but it was pointless to give way to childish temper now ... In another half an hour she would be rid of him. All she had to do was to concentrate on the landscape and pretend that it was someone else sitting there beside her.

# CHAPTER FIVE

THE car tyres crunched steadily over the gravel drive as Dominic turned in through the gates to the house, the sound unnaturally loud in the thick silence inside the vehicle. He brought it to a standstill next to the front door. As she reached for the door handle, at the same time releasing her seatbelt, she felt his hand on her arm. Apprehension feathered coldly along her skin, but she didn't look at him, or acknowledge his touch in any way.

'I want to talk to you.'

So that was it. What did he want to say that hadn't been said eight years ago?

Pain made her lash out with childish venom, her voice high and shaky as she threw back acidly, 'Well, I didn't suppose you were giving me a lift out of sheer human charity!'

'Very wise of you. Shall we go inside?'

Kate didn't want to invite him into the house ... didn't want to see him in those same surroundings ... but something told her that he was not going to allow her to refuse.

Her whole body felt stiff and unfamiliar as she unlocked the door and walked into the hall. She paused by the drawing-room door, and saw his face darken slightly, as though he too were remembering. She shuddered slightly, and saw that his eyes had registered her faint movement. They glowed dark topaz, hot instead of cold,

tracking her every movement ... waiting for her
to ... to what?

Impatient of the theatrical direction of her
thoughts, she pushed open the drawing-room
door and walked inside.

Strategically she stood behind one of the
chairs, holding on to the back as she turned to
face him, and demanded coldly:

'Now, what is it you wanted to say to me?'

It was disconcerting to find Dominic standing
so close to her, close enough for her to see the
faint lines raying out from his eyes that were new
to her from eight years ago. Time had hardened
him, it seemed, or at least, she amended mentally,
it had stripped away the veneer of compassion
she had once foolishly deceived herself he
possessed, to reveal his true nature. There was
certainly no warmth in the topaz eyes fixed on
her own. Strange that such a warm colour as gold
could look so cold.

Of course, if Vera was to be believed, and Kate
had to admit she could see no reason for her to
lie, Dominic did have some justification for
mistrusting the female sex. However, mistrust
was one thing, dislike to the point of wanting to
hurt was another.

There was such an air of taut control about
him that she badly wanted to step back, but pride
compelled her to stay where she was, her chin
tilting slightly as her eyes clashed with his. She
was not twenty any more, looking hopelessly for
the love she had been denied by her husband,
desperate to prove her femininity.

'I don't know why you're so anxious to

cultivate Vera Benson,' Dominic said harshly at last, 'but if it's Ian you're after, you're wasting your time. He's devoted to Vera . . . far too much to be taken in by someone like you.'

Somehow Kate managed to contain her outrage long enough to say icily, 'I am *not* cultivating Vera, as you put it, but I do have my living to earn, and . . .'

'You expect me to believe that?' His mouth curled unpleasantly as he looked towards the gardens beyond the drawing-room's french windows. 'I doubt if what you earn brings in enough to keep so much as a gardener for this place!'

Once again Kate was amazed at her own self-control. It was almost as though she were standing outside herself in some way, more of an onlooker than a participant in what was going on.

'You're quite right,' she told him coolly. 'Which is why I'm putting the house up for sale. My father left me a small cottage a few miles away, and I intend to move into that. Not that it's any business of yours.' She gave him an icy smile and with regal disdain added, 'Now, if you would kindly leave——'

'My, my, how cool and controlled you've become!' Dominic's voice was light, tinged with mocking amusement, his expression deceptively relaxed, but Kate was not deceived. She had seen his eyes before he veiled them with the thickness of his lashes to hide the rage burning darkly there.

Against her will she experienced a tremor of fear, a nameless apprehension that touched some deeply feminine part of her.

'But you weren't so cool or indifferent eight years ago, were you, Kate? When you pleaded with me to make love to you . . .'

Her control snapping, Kate launched herself at him slapping his face so hard that her palm stung, shocking her out of her momentary madness to the disquieting realisation that what she had done in some way had pleased him. She could see it in the savage glitter of triumph in his eyes, and once more fear iced along her spine.

She wanted to turn and run; to hide herself away from him, and she wished she had given in to that impulse when suddenly he reached for her, lifting her off her feet, despite her height, carrying her through the door and up the stairs, in spite of her frenzied attempts to break free of him.

His fingers bit painfully into her skin as he used his foot to push open the door to the guest room.

Rage and something else, alien and disconcerting, glittered in his eyes as he dropped her on the bed so carelessly that momentarily she was too winded and shocked to do more than simply glare up at him, her body strangely weak.

Her weakness only lasted a second though before she was struggling to sit up, her sharp cry of fury muffled by the fierce pressure of Dominic's mouth against her own, the weight of his body pressing her back against the mattress, his fingers locking like manacles round her slender wrists.

When he had kissed her before he had shocked and disillusioned her, hurt her badly, physically as well as mentally, and although she could sense that same savagery pent up inside him now, it was not fear, but a shocking, racing excitement that flooded through her body, holding her immobile beneath the bruising heat of his kiss.

Under her thin T-shirt and equally thin bra she could feel her breasts responding to the hardness of the muscled chest pressed against them, her nipples tingling, aching with an intensity she had never known as a naïve bride, but which she easily recognised now as the onset of overwhelming desire.

She could not want him . . . not this man . . . It was . . . it was sick, she told herself, hating what he was doing to her senses, hating the way she ached to fling off her clothes and his to have the male heat of his skin caressing her own.

'Kate . . .' Her name sounded unfamiliar to her as she caught the inarticulate mutter he made against her mouth, her throat aching in response to the raw need dammed up behind that single yearning sound.

She was going mad, she told herself bitterly as his mouth returned to hers, more delicately this time, probing, tasting, exploring . . . Dominic hated and despised her, she knew that.

So why was he kissing her? Why . . .?

'Why are you doing this?' She didn't recognise the husky words as coming from her own throat until Dominic raised his head to look at her. She saw his mouth thin as he laughed bitterly, and knew she had been mad to think his feelings towards her might somehow have changed.

'Why?'

He lifted his head to look down into her face and as she stared into his eyes Kate felt her heart contract painfully. Numbly she recognised that she had been a fool to think she could ignore this man or remain indifferent to him. He might not possess all the virtues with which she had invested him eight years ago, but he did possess something that drew her to him; something that made her ache and long to recklessly deny the question she had just asked; to blot out her knowledge of the truth and the burning self-disgust she could see quite plainly in his eyes and to think only instead of the desire that leaped tumultuously between them, but it was already too late . . . as he repeated with raw incredulity, 'Why? Oh, come on, Kate, you aren't that naïve! Far from it. I wanted you eight years ago, and I want you now.'

It was the last thing she had expected to hear and momentarily she was stunned by it, the protest rising to her lips, her instinctive denial silenced as he continued harshly,

'I don't make love to other men's wives, Kate, no matter how tempted I am . . . and God knows I was.'

She saw the expression in his eyes and shrank from the pain of it, knowing now why his dislike and contempt of her was so intense. He might want her, but he resented that wanting, Kate could see that clearly.

'For eight long years you've haunted me, Kate. You'll never know how many nights I've lain alone in my bed cursing myself for being a fool to turn down what you offered.' His mouth twisted in the way she was beginning to recognise. 'At least I was an honourable fool, and I've no illusions about how quickly you found someone less ... scrupulous ... to take the place I refused.'

'You want me?' Her thoughts were a seething mass of contradictions, but the trite words were all she could think of to say.

'Yes, much to my disgust. I shouldn't be telling you this, should I? No doubt it gives you a great deal of amusement to know how much I desire you, totally against my will ...'

'If you've wanted me so much then why wait so long?' she asked quietly, watching him. 'Ricky's been dead for over six years now.'

'I didn't know. I've been living and working in New York, don't forget,' he told her harshly. 'What happened, Kate?' He expelled his breath painfully, his chest expanding and contracting against the pressure of his almost physical anguish. 'Did your faithlessness eventually kill him?'

It came to her then that far from pitying herself, all her pity ought to be reserved for Dominic. Almost gently she reached up, to smooth the thick damp hair back off his forehead. He was sweating heavily, like someone deep in the grip of a powerful fever, his eyes overbright and his skin hot. Almost as though she herself were somehow removed from their small personal drama, she found herself judicially assessing and weighing his emotions. Was it the torment of desiring *her*, a woman whom he felt he should despise, that had carved those lines on his face?

That he was telling her the truth she did not for one moment doubt, but instead of feeling the sharp pleasure of revenge, all she could feel was a terrible, silencing pity.

Here was a man who through his own blindness had put himself on a rack of torture. A man who had misjudged her so badly that she still hurt from the wounds he had inflicted, and yet who in inflicting them had hurt himself far more.

The thought of telling him the truth never even crossed her mind. The desire for him that had burned through her so hotly only minutes ago had now cooled. He wanted her ... but against his will ... against everything he believed in, and his wanting for her was a sickness, a flaw in himself as far as he was concerned.

He wasn't holding her as tightly as he had been and it was easy to wriggle out from beneath him and get off the bed.

'Kate ...' Dominic reached out for her, but she evaded him, standing looking down into his face and reading the agony there. Part of her wanted to reach out to touch him; to stop his pain, but logic told her that that was impossible. Just as she had had to search inside herself for release from the misery he had caused her, so too must he find his own panacea for his ailment.

'I think you'd better go, Dominic.'

She said it without emotion, standing to one side as he rolled off the bed and stood up.

In silence they went downstairs together, stopping only in the hall when Dominic grabbed her arm, swinging her round to face him.

'You wanted me,' he told her rawly. 'I don't

know why you changed your mind, Kate, but you wanted me and I could have made you go on wanting me.'

She didn't deny it, but said instead with a faintly wintry smile, 'Think of it as an act of contrition then on my part, Dominic. After all, I've just saved you from yourself, haven't I? Some people enjoy wanting what hurts them most,' she added softly.

She saw his face drain of colour, but suppressed her sympathy for him. Given what Vera had told her about his childhood wasn't it possible that in some way he desired her because in his eyes she was the same sort of woman as the mother who had deserted his father, and moreover that he had felt bound to punish himself for that desire? Telling herself that she was venturing into extremely murky and unknown waters, Kate gently pulled her arm free and went to open the front door.

He walked through it without a word.

A full hour after he had left Kate was still sitting curled up in the chair in the library, gazing pensively into the unlit fire, trying to come to terms with what she had learned.

What Dominic had said to her put a completely different light on what had happened that fateful weekend when she had invited him to make love to her. The harsh rejection she had found so bitterly painful she now saw as a denial directed as much at himself as at her, and no doubt if she had been as experienced as he believed her to be, she would have realised the truth then. But what good would realising it have done?

It would have spared her years of torment, believing herself to be totally undesirable to the male sex. But it wasn't only Dominic's rejection of her that had made her so aloof and distant with men, she knew that. And the proof that Dominic had not destroyed her ability to respond sexually given the right incentive, lay in the way she had felt in his arms today. It was useless to hide from herself the fact that she had wanted him; that he aroused within her a deeply passionate response, so intense that it overruled everything else. But it was a desire that was best left unfulfilled, and it came to her as she sat there, that part of the reason she was not going to tell Dominic the truth about herself was because she saw his contempt of her and hatred of himself as a form of protection. She was frightened of how she might feel about him if that barrier was removed. Life with Ricky had destroyed her trust in men, her ability to believe she was worthy of their love, and that had not changed. Dominic might desire, but he did not and could not ever love her, while she ... She froze back into the chair as the unpalatable, devastating truth slid into her mind. She was all too capable of loving him. Once acknowledged, such a truth could not be hidden away again. If she was honest she would have to admit that she had fallen in love with him eight years ago ... hopelessly and painfully, without even knowing what sort of man he was. And that love would grow, she recognised that now, which was why it was imperative that she kept him at a distance.

Her heartbeat thundered in her own ears as she tried to calculate how long she would be able to keep him at bay. Today she had been able to dismiss him, but how long did she have before that dark, fierce desire she sensed in him overturned the control of his mind and he made good the words he had said to her before he left. It would not be a matter of using force, both of them knew that. All he needed to do was to touch her and her self-control vanished.

Very well then, she told herself resolutely, she would just have to see that he never got the opportunity to touch her. As she made this decision the thought slid into her mind that if Dominic were to believe she had another lover . . . But that was impossible.

Work was the only panacea she could find, and she used it ruthlessly to blot out all thoughts of Dominic. She was lucky, she told herself tiredly as she let herself into the house late one afternoon, that the setting up of her new partnership with Harry meant that she was having to make constant trips to her solicitor and the bank.

She had been surprised by how well the bank manager had received her request for a loan. She had explained to him that she was going to sell the house and he had gone through her financial circumatances in thorough detail with her.

Harry too had been able to secure a loan, and their new partnership would be official from the end of the month.

Today she had been to London with Harry to

the workshop off the docks to tell the others
about their plans which had been greeted with
pleasing enthusiasm. If she could just get a
commission from Vera now the new venture
would be off to a flying start.

It was a nuisance that she was still without a
car, but the garage had promised to get hers back
to her just as soon as they could, although they
had told her that its roadworthy life was now
extremely limited.

The phone rang as she walked inside and her
stomach jolted treacherously, but it wasn't
Dominic, it was the estate agent, suggesting that
he call round in the morning to assess the house.

They had been having a spell of exceptionally
good weather, and in the morning, to take
advantage of the slight breeze, Kate wedged the
front door open so that the air could waft through
the house. The estate agent was due at ten, and
then she was going over to have lunch with Sue.
The summer heat called for cool easy-to-wear
clothes and on impulse she had bought herself a
new dress when she was in London.

It had been so long since she had last bought
herself anything new that she had been faintly
shocked by the prices, but a cheque received the
previous day for some work she had done had
made her feel reckless. It was a pleasant feeling to
spend money she had earned herself, and in the
end she had surprised herself by buying a totally
unsuitable but undeniably lovely concoction
which consisted of two tiers of finely pleated cool
white cotton chiffon below the waist while above
it, the cotton chiffon was supplemented by two

panels of delicate blue and green embroidery on a white background which ran from the small round neckline down to the softly bloused waist at both the front and the back. Long full sleeves in the white cotton chiffon fastened at the wrists with another band of embroidery, and while a streak of common sense had told her that the dress was an unnecessary luxury, Kate hadn't been able to resist it.

Now the fabric felt deliciously cool against her skin, and catching sight of herself in a mirror she paused to study her reflection more thoroughly. Despite its demure high neck and long sleeves the dress had a floaty, almost transparent quality that hinted erotically at the shape of the body it clothed. The delicate tones of the embroidery highlighted her vivid colouring, and her hair, newly washed and totally untameable, had for once been left down.

The dress was, Kate recognised wryly, the representation of a female urge as old as time, that of needing to make herself as attractive as possible to the man she desired. But hadn't she already decided that she was going to do all she could to discourage Dominic?

The sound of a car coming up the drive put an end to her musings and she got downstairs just in time to greet the estate agent as he stepped out of his car.

'Martin Allwood, Mrs Hammond,' he introduced himself, extending his hand. 'We did meet when you came into the office.'

His fair hair glinted in the sun, his expression openly admiring as light blue eyes studied her tall slender body.

'If I may say so, you present a charmingly cool appearance on a very hot morning.'

'I'm due to have lunch with a friend,' Kate responded coolly, warning him that she had not dressed for his benefit, and the interest in his eyes sharpened slightly.

'I think if you don't mind we'll do the garden first,' he suggested. 'There's much more land with the property than I had realised. It would make an ideal family home—just the sort I'd like myself, if I was married . . .'

Kate, falling into step with him as they followed the crazy paving path round the side of the house, looked sharply at him, wondering if he was deliberately informing her that he wasn't married. He was attractive enough, although a little too bland and squeaky-clean for her taste, but she had no doubt that most women found him attractive.

They went over the garden and then through the house, Kate answering his questions about the history of the house. He had discarded the jacket of his suit, after asking her permission, and unfastened the top buttons of his shirt.

They had reached the main bedroom when Kate heard another car coming down the drive. Frowning slightly for she wasn't expecting anyone, she went to the window and leaned out, her frown lifting as she saw that it was her own car. The garage had obviously finished working on it and had brought it back for her.

Obviously drawn to the window by the new arrival, Martin Allwood came to stand behind her, one arm extended behind her to support himself as he too leaned forward.

The car door opened, and Kate felt her stomach cramp protestingly as Dominic got out.

He looked up at the window straight away, and it was only when she saw his mouth compress that Kate realised that the way they were standing suggested an intimacy between herself and the estate agent that actually had no reality.

'I'd better go down,' she told him as they both moved away from the window.

'I'll follow you ... there isn't much more for me to do up here ... this was the last room, wasn't it?'

Nodding her agreement, Kate hurried downstairs. She had left the front door open and Dominic was standing in the hall, his face contorted with savage anger.

'What have you done with your lover?' he demanded harshly. 'Left him to finish dressing on his own? You're being very indiscreet entertaining him so early in the day, Kate. Does he know, I wonder, that he's satisfying a desire I aroused in you?'

The bitter mingling of anger and contempt, his totally erroneous suppositions about her, took Kate's breath away for a moment. It was ridiculous that Dominic should think that she and Martin Allwood were lovers ... and she opened her mouth to tell him so when she realised what he had said about her desire for him, and anger replaced her stupefaction.

'You're very arrogant, Dominic,' she told him softly, veiling her eyes with her lashes before he could see the gleam of temper in them. 'You're not the only man I've wanted, you know.'

She hadn't expected her gibe to have the effect it did. Almost immediately the bitterness died from his eye, to be replaced by pain. He took a step towards her and then stopped, looking at the stairs. Glancing over her shoulder, Kate saw Martin Allwood coming leisurely down the stairs, shrugging on his jacket as he did so, for all the world as though he were indeed perhaps her lover.

As she turned away from Dominic to follow him outside to his car, he said to her with a smile, 'I'll be in touch as soon as I can.'

He got into his car and was just about to drive off when Dominic walked up to it and asked casually, 'If you're going back in the direction of the village, I wonder if I might beg a lift. I left my own car at the garage.'

'Sure . . . Get in.'

Her forehead creased in a frown, Kate watched them drive away. Why had Dominic begged a lift from Martin? To warn him about the sort of woman she was? She went cold at the thought, but could not think of any other reason for his behaviour. It was obvious to her that having brought out her car he must have expected that she would drive him back to the garage . . . but he had gone almost without exchanging a word with her.

As always, Sue was pleased to see her, commenting appreciatively on how attractive she looked.

'Obviously you're not letting what Dominic said get to you. Good for you, Kate, it's high time you started living again. By the way,' she added curiously, 'you never did say why he reacted to you the way he did.'

The secret Kate had guarded so assiduously in the past no longer seemed so important and so, taking a deep breath, she explained to her friend what had happened that fateful weekend.

'And he rejected you?' Sue asked, saucer-eyed.

'He thought I made a habit of going to bed with all and sundry,' Kate told Sue drily, 'but it's all in the past now.'

'Well, I must say you're taking it all very philosophically,' Sue marvelled. 'In your shoes ... well, I'd certainly like to give him a taste of his own medicine at the very least!'

Although she had told Sue everything that had happened eight years ago, Kate had not told her that she now knew that Dominic desired her, nor did she intend to; it would complicate the issue too much, and besides, she had no wish to expose him. On the contrary, she actually felt faintly protective towards him, wanting to shield him.

'It's over now and totally unimportant,' she told Sue lazily.

'But to criticise you like that, and in public ...' protested Sue, growing quite heated again. 'Honestly, Kate, you should have told him the truth ... taken him down a peg or two. I've invited the Bensons over for lunch on Sunday. I could have a word with Vera, if you like...'

'No ... honestly, I'd rather leave it,' Kate told her, glancing at her watch and announcing that it was time she was on her way.

'Well, don't forget, we expect you for lunch as

well on Sunday,' Sue reminded her as she walked her to her car. 'I hope this weather holds, I thought we might have a barbecue outside ... what do you think?'

'I think it's a good idea, the forecast is promising.'

'Mmm.'

They kissed and Kate got in her car. Sue was a dear and loyal friend, if inclined to be a little hot-tempered, she thought with a grin as she drove off, but the last thing she wanted now was for Dominic to know the truth—although even if he did know would he be able to accept it?

She took a different route home than usual to save time, one she rarely used because she did not like it. The road ran past the grim bulk of a high-security prison, and every time Kate saw it it made her shiver. What must it be like to be locked up inside there for the rest of one's life? And yet weren't even many people who were physically free still prisoners, locked up within their own emotional problems? Just as she had been locked up in the fear of her own inadequacy as a woman ... just as Dominic was locked up in his struggle between wanting her and despising her.

Sighing faintly, she automatically increased her speed a little as she drove past the prison.

There had been a tremendous amount of local opposition to it when it had been built twenty years ago. Both her father and Ricky's grandfather had objected strenuously to it, since it was closer to their homes than it was to the village, but their objections had not prevailed.

The restlessness which had possessed her since Dominic's reappearance in her life consumed her that evening. She wandered out into the garden, suddenly realising that she was still wearing her new dress. Why? It was the sort of dress a woman wore for a man . . . but she had no man to wear it for . . . nor wanted one, she told herself fiercely.

The heat of the day had given way to an oppressive over-warm evening, with the promise of the sort of night that made sleep impossible.

Kate was just considering the virtues of a cooling shower when the phone rang.

Picking up the receiver, she recognised Vera's voice, bubbling with excitement and pleasure.

'Kate, Ian's agreed to your design for the conservatory!' she began without preamble. 'I'm so thrilled, I had to ring and tell you right away. He loved the design right from the start, but he took a bit of convincing over the cost.' Vera gave a rich chuckle. 'But now that he and Dominic have agreed the last details of their merger, he's a little more relaxed. I was wondering if I could come over and see you so that we could discuss the design in more detail?'

When Kate replaced the receiver, tempering her delight that Vera had offered her the commission was the knowledge that Dominic might be about to become a more permanent feature of local life than she had envisaged. Still, she comforted herself that he would want to be involved with her as little as she did with him. His desire for her was purely physical, tormenting him all the more because he felt he should not want her, and who could tell, now, believing that

Martin Allwood was her lover, might he not decide that he did not want her after all?

Logic told Kate that a man who on his admission had wanted her for eight years was hardly likely to suddenly cease that wanting ... but it was a logic she didn't want to hear.

# CHAPTER NINE

On the Friday morning Martin Allwood rang to discuss with Kate the price he thought she should ask for the property. It was very much higher than she had expected, but he explained to her that he thought it highly likely that it would be bought by one of the many London-based businessmen moving into the area.

'We could have asked another three or four thousand,' he continued, 'but in view of the proximity of the prison I decided against it. There are those who would consider that, plus the relative remoteness of the house, a negative factor,' he warned her. 'It's not exactly unknown for prisoners to break out of these places, and the house is pretty close by. However, I don't think we need to concern ourselves too much about that.' He paused and then added quickly, 'I was wondering whether I could take you out for lunch on Sunday ... it's the only day we don't work during the summer and ...'

Thankful that she had a genuine excuse, Kate refused, explaining that she was already committed to lunch with someone else, and since Martin did not press the issue, she suspected it was the sort of invitation he made casually to every woman who took his eye.

It was only later that she called herself a fool for not taking what would have been a golden

opportunity to provide herself with a genuine
barrier against Dominic, but it was too late for
second thoughts now.

Saturday she spent with Harry, going round
some of the churches under his care. Together
they inspected their stained glass, Kate making
notes for later on. This more traditional aspect of
their work was not as interesting to her as the
more modern commissions, but it all provided
valuable experience, and she couldn't help
marvelling at the details that had gone into some
of the windows. In many cases they were already
damaged with pieces missing, but they could be
repaired, and it was good to have something that
would bring in a regular source of income.

'Same time next week,' joked Harry as she left
for home. 'We've still got a dozen or so to do.'

'Fine,' Kate agreed. 'I'll get these notes typed
up and make out a folder for them.'

'Very businesslike,' Harry teased her, adding
wryly as she started her car, 'And take care, I
don't like you driving that old banger all the way
over here, Kate ... I think I could swing it so
that you could get a loan from the bank to buy a
new one.'

Touched by his thoughtfulness, she shook her
head. 'It's okay,' she assured him. 'I'm planning
to change it once the house is sold, which
shouldn't take too long. Which reminds me ...
I'd like you to come over and have a look at the
cottage with me. It's got some outhouses, which I
thought could be converted into a workshop, but
I'll need your advice.'

'Mmm ... sounds good. A second workshop

would be very useful. Give me a ring when you want me to come over.' Harry bent to kiss her cheek and then stood watching until she had driven out of sight.

Harry made her feel warm and cared for, Kate thought happily as she headed for home. In some ways he and his family had become her own, replacing the father she had lost and the mother she had never really known, but as yet she hadn't told him about Dominic ...

But then what was there to tell? Nothing, she told herself firmly, and that was the way it was going to stay.

Kate prepared for Sue's lunch with lethargic indifference, knowing she did not want to go, but also knowing that Sue would cross-question her if she did not.

The good weather was holding, heat rippling the tarmac as she drove towards her friend's, reminding her of how, as a child, she would sit in the back seat of her father's car with her nose glued to the window, until the undulating road surface was transformed into water.

Reminding herself of how dangerous it was to let her mind wander when she was driving, she banished the childhood memory. The sunshine had filled the roads with drivers, and she was glad when she was finally able to turn off into the road that led to her friend's home.

The first thing she saw as she turned into the drive was a silver-grey BMW, and her heart leapt frantically in a complex mixture of pleasure and fear, until she realised that the one Dominic had been driving had been a different colour, and that this one must belong to the Bensons.

She was familiar enough with her friend's home not to need to ring the bell, but to make her way round the side of the house to the large patio at the back, where, as she had expected, she found her host and hostess.

John was bending over a portable barbecue fiddling with something while Sue stood to one side.

The children saw Kate first, abandoning their game to rush over to her, hugging her legs enthusiastically.

The commotion made Sue look up and grin in welcome.

'We're just having our usual battle with the barbecue,' she announced cheerfully. 'John swears that I deliberately put a hex on it. It will never burn properly if you put so much charcoal on it,' she protested, turning back to her husband, adding to Kate, 'Honestly, men! If John left it to me to light . . . Why on earth does anything to do with making things burn fascinate men so much?'

Her last question was directed at Kate, but it was John who answered it, having successfully ignited the charcoal, his hazel eyes gleaming with amusement as he hugged her briefly and said, 'It's part of man's age-old instinct to protect and succour his womenfolk . . . keeping the home fires burning . . . all that sort of thing.'

'It was women who kept the home fires burning,' Sue retorted, reaching up to wipe a smut of charcoal dust from his cheek.

Watching them, Kate was filled with a raw, aching pain caused by the knowledge that she would never know that closeness, that sense of togetherness and sharing that existed between Sue and John.

Before their marriage, Sue had trained as a nurse, and had gone on to qualify as a midwife before having her children, and Kate knew that John respected her in a professional capacity in addition to loving her as a woman.

Kate did not make the mistake of viewing her friends' marriage through a rose-coloured veil. It was not idyllic, Sue often complained that there were times when she felt frustrated and angry that her skills were not being put to use, but on the other hand, she felt that while they were young the children needed her, and also as a local G.P., John needed her to be at home to take his calls, and generally act as an unpaid assistant. Sue had confided to Kate in the early days after she had had the children that she felt there was something essentially diminishing about being reliant on someone else financially having earned her own living, even though John was a generous and thoughtful husband, but on balance, their relationship worked in a way that any relationship between herself and Dominic never could.

For a start he didn't have an ounce of respect for her as a person. He wanted her only as a physical entity without knowing or wanting to know the woman she actually was. While she . . .

She was drawn to him in a way that she knew was dangerous. Where she should have felt anger and resentment, she felt compassion and sorrow.

It hurt her that he should so desperately have hurt himself, and all so needlessly. She could understand how a father could influence and poison a child's mind against the female sex, but surely, as an adult, Dominic must have come to the realisation that his father's views were very one-sided?

'Ian and Vera are looking at the garden,' Sue announced, breaking into her thoughts. 'They're a very pleasant couple, don't you think?' She made a small moue. 'I was a bit anti at first; incomers and all that ... but the more I see of them the more I like them. Did you know that Ian's business is merging with Dominic's?'

'Yes. Vera told me.'

Sue made another face. 'Now there's someone I can't take to, not after the way he insulted you.'

'Stop bristling,' teased John, catching the tail of what she was saying, adding to Kate with a wry grin, 'To look at her you'd never think she was such a fierce little thing, would you?' He tugged Sue's fair hair, looking at her with affection. 'When she was on the wards, senior consultants used to tremble with fear!'

'Oh, you ...' Sue gave her husband a little push. 'I think the barbecue's ready for the steaks. Could you give me a hand bringing out the salad?' she asked Kate.

They were in the kitchen before Sue resumed the conversation John had interrupted, beginning, 'As I was just saying, I'm getting very fond of the Bensons, Vera in particular, which makes it all the more ...' She broke off, as she looked through the kitchen window. 'They're coming back now. Kate, believe me this wasn't my idea, but when they arrived Dominic was with them.'

Kate was glad that she had her back to her friend. Her whole system seemed to have gone into civil war. After that first thrill of seeing what she had thought was Dominic's car in the drive she had been relieved by the knowledge that it wasn't, and yet here was Sue telling her that he was here after all.

'Don't worry about it.' She marvelled at how calm her voice sounded. 'I'll take these out, shall I?' She picked up two large bowls of salad, avoiding her friend's eyes, determined not to betray anything of what she felt inside.

Vera and Ian both greeted her warmly, Dominic either strategically or accidentally was busily involved with the children, and by the time Ian had finished quizzing her about the expense of the stained glass Vera had commissioned, her tension was beginning to ease slightly.

Even so it was impossible for her to eat much, and when she sat down she made sure it was as far away from Dominic as possible. If she hadn't been so tense and on edge, she might almost have been amused at Sue's role reversal. Where in the past her friend had always been eager to bring her to the attention of any unattached males she invited round, today she was behaving like the very strictest kind of duenna, protectively making sure that Dominic was never allowed to come so much as within speaking distance of her.

He seemed to have lost weight, and despite his tan, he did not look well. Her heart ached for him and yet at the same time she was conscious of a terrible feeling of hopelessness.

What should have been a pleasantly relaxed lunch was a nightmare of strain and anguish. As soon as she safely could she stood up and pinned a bright smile to her lips.

Anticipating her, Sue frowned and exclaimed, 'You're not going so soon, are you?' The glare she directed towards Dominic's stiff back made it plain that she knew where the blame for this lay, and unwillingly Kate looked at him too.

Dressed in jeans and a thin short-sleeved cotton shirt, he looked more human ... more vulnerable than when she had seen him before. The jeans hugged his legs and thighs, but were slightly loose on the waist, the shirt taut over the defensively hunched contours of his back. She wanted to go up to him and wrap her arms protectively around him, to ease away his pain, but how could she when she herself was the cause of it?

He turned round, unexpectedly catching her looking at him, and his eyes darkened, making desire tremble to life inside her. If only she could just give in to that aching, melting flare of need, but at twenty-seven one could not blot out the realities of life so easily.

'Oh, Kate, must you really leave?' Vera asked regretfully.

Out of the corner of her eye Kate saw Dominic's mouth twist, his voice so harsh that it shivered painfully through her too vulnerable skin as he interrupted curtly, 'No doubt she has a date with her estate agent friend . . .'

'A date?' Sue ignored Dominic to turn a pleased face towards her friend. 'Kate, and you never said! Where's he taking you?'

Not knowing what on earth she could say without telling a lie, Kate hesitated, and then into the silence as devastatingly shocking to the senses as hearing an unexpected gun go off she heard Dominic saying *sotto voce*, 'About as far as the nearest bed, I should imagine.'

Kate knew that the taunt was meant only for her, but Sue was standing so close to her, she heard it too, and temper ignited in her eyes as she looked from Kate's white face to Dominic's implacable one.

Sensing an imminent explosion, Kate took hold of her arm, squeezing it warningly as she said, 'Come with me to the car.'

She could sense that Sue was torn, but John, Vera and Ian were all engrossed in conversation and unwillingly Sue allowed herself to be drawn away, giving vent to her feelings only once they were safely out of earshot of the others.

'That man really is the end!' she exploded angrily. 'Honestly, Kate . . .'

'Forget it.' Kate managed to smile, 'I don't even have a date with Martin Allwood.'

'Martin Allwood?' asked Sue, diverted. 'I know him. Very up-and-coming, isn't he, and very attractive? How did you get to meet him?'

'He came to assess the house. You know I'm putting it up for sale. Dominic brought my car back and saw us both at an upstairs window.' Kate pulled a wry face. 'And of course he immediately jumped to the wrong conclusion.'

'Mmm ... it seems to me that that gentleman has a history of jumping to wrong conclusions, especially where you're concerned.'

Sue stood in the drive until Kate's car had disappeared, and then made her way back to her remaining guests.

'Kate got off safely, did she?' her husband asked, sliding a fond arm round her waist. 'That old banger of hers isn't very reliable . . .'

'I know, she's planning to replace it just as soon as the house is sold.'

He saw that his wife's eyes were not on him, but on the back of the man walking down their garden.

'Forget it, love,' he advised softly, following her thoughts.

'But, John, he was so nasty to her ... Kate's had enough to endure. It makes my blood boil to hear him sniping at her like that!'

'Yes, I know, but there's nothing we can do about it, love.'

John might think that, but she certainly didn't, Sue thought, watching Dominic disappearing through the arch in the rose hedge which led to the old-fashioned orchard.

Slipping away from her husband, and using Vera and Ian to decoy him with their plans for The Grange, she followed Dominic down to the orchard.

He was leaning against the trunk of a plum tree, hands in the pockets of his jeans as he stared at the ground. His smile for her was polite, but wary. He was an exceedingly attractive man, Sue thought dispassionately, but she preferred her John every day of the week.

A very fierce loyalty to her family and friends
was one of the cornerstones of Sue's personality,
coupled with a deep-rooted sense of fair play
which in her youth had led her into more than
one turbulent situation. She could never bear to
see anyone being done down unfairly, and least of
all her dearest friend. When she thought of the
life Kate had endured with Ricky! The light of
battle glittered in her eyes as she took a step
towards her victim.

Without preamble she said firmly, 'I'd like to
have a word with you.'

At another time she might have been flattered
by the amused and warm smile that curved his
mouth, instantly transforming him, but on this
occasion she had other things on her mind.

'I don't know why you seem to have set
yourself up as the judge of Kate's morality,
but . . .'

He cut her off immediately, almost brutally,
the smile dying to be placed by a wall of cold
disdain as he interrupted,

'I understand that Kate is your friend, but you
must realise that Ricky was mine.'

Sue didn't let him get any further, her temper
overwhelming caution as she exclaimed heatedly,

'Oh, was he? Was he really? Well, do you *know*
what your *friend* did to Kate? Do you? Did you
know that he married her knowing that he didn't
love her, and with no intention of even trying to
love her? Did you *know* that he deliberately
encouraged her to think he was in love with her?
He was twenty-seven years old then, she was an
immature seventeen-year-old who'd just lost her

father and been told by her mother that there was
no home for her with her in America. Kate
thought Ricky loved her when he married her,
but she soon discovered otherwise—and believe
me, never once during the farce that her marriage
was did she ever so much as say one word against
him. It was only when she finally broke down
when he was killed—killed while with another
woman, I might add—that she finally admitted to
me just what her marriage had been.

'Systematically and vindictively Ricky tried to
destroy her as a woman. After the first few weeks
of their marriage he never once made love to her
... he told her that he had no desire for her, that
she was incapable of arousing desire in any man.'
Sue broke off for a moment, seeing the way
Dominic's face paled, but any pity she might
have felt was swamped by her burning need to
vindicate her friend.

'And of course Kate believed him, because
after all, didn't she have ample proof that Ricky
could be aroused—by almost every other female
he saw? He was consistently unfaithful to Kate
right from the start of their marriage, sometimes
staying away for days at a time. He married her
because he wanted the land her father had left
her, and because her mother promised him an
allowance for as long as the marriage lasted.

'Kate told me that once she knew the truth, she
asked him for a divorce, but he refused to give
her one.' Sue saw Dominic's mouth open and
rushed on hotly, 'And you needn't think that by
telling me about that weekend when Kate tried to
seduce you, you're going to shock me. I know all

about it—Kate told me the other day.' Her mouth curled, her eyes condemning.

'Dear God, what kind of man are you that you couldn't see the truth for yourself? Instead of giving her the comfort and reassurance she so badly needed, you only reinforced all the doubts she had about herself. You made her hate herself, did you know that? She's lived like a hermit since Ricky died. And don't start thinking that I'm making any of this up. Ask anyone in the village, they all know what Ricky was like.'

The force of her emotions made tears burn in her eyes, her voice shaking as she flung at him, 'No doubt you're very proud of the high moral stand you've taken . . . of the constant taunts you fling at Kate, but I think of you as criminally foolish—and arrogant. Blind as well, for not being able to see the obvious!'

Suddenly and inexplicably she had run out of steam, and even more extraordinarily when she looked into his face and saw the expression there, the anger that had fired her was gone. She started to move away and Dominic reached out to stop her.

'Please . . . please tell me all this again. Slowly this time, from the beginning.'

Perhaps he wasn't quite the villain she had imagined after all, Sue thought, noting the expression in his eyes. After all, what could not be excused as the reaction of an indifferent observer could be viewed in a completely different light as the behaviour of a would-be lover.

She sat down on the grass and patted a spot

beside her. Dominic sat down beside her, and starting right from the beginning she told him the history of Kate's marriage.

After leaving Sue's, Kate drove straight home, but once there she could not settle. A restless, yearning energy seemed to possess her, her thoughts constantly circling around Dominic. At last, knowing that only strenuous physical activity could dissipate her tension, she collected some cleaning articles and her keys and drove down to the cottage.

Her first task was to open all the windows and get rid of the stale, cloying atmosphere inside.

Although described as a cottage, in reality it was a small house. Downstairs there was a pleasant sitting-room with windows overlooking both front and back; a hall; a dining-room which her father had used as a study, and a large sunny kitchen.

Upstairs there were three good sized bedrooms, one with its own shower, and a separate bathroom.

The gardens were of a more manageable size than those attached to the house, mostly laid down to lawns attractively broken up by borders bursting with cottage garden plants, and the odd rockery islands smothered in creeping plants.

While she waited for the immersion to heat enough water for her to start cleaning, Kate went over the house. It was strange how those things which had once been so familiar to her now seemed slightly alien. This had been her home for almost eighteen years; the shabby furniture that she had grown up with. All the rooms needed redecorating, she noticed. If she could spare the time between commissions, she might do it herself. She had helped Sue to do the children's room the previous winter and had thoroughly enjoyed it. It struck her as she went back to the kitchen that at twenty-seven she had never really had a home of her own. This cottage had belonged to her father; the house she now lived in had been Ricky's and before him his grandfather's, and even though she loved it she had never felt moved to stamp her own personality on it.

By the time she had scrubbed the kitchen from top to bottom, she felt tired enough to call it a day.

Outside dusk was starting to fall, making her realise that she had been at the cottage far longer than she had anticipated. Stretching her aching back, she packed away her cleaning things, noting ruefully how wet her jeans had become. They clung clammily to her legs, uncomfortably so, as she drove home.

As she walked up to the door the darkness and silence that greeted her suddenly made her feel terribly alone. A dull melancholy feeling, in tune with the growing dusk, enveloped her as she contrasted her lifestyle with Sue's. She had promised herself long ago that she would never allow herself to be envious of women who had what she did not, but tonight the emptiness of the house depressed her, bringing back bitter-sharp memories of how she had felt on first coming to this house as a bride, and how she had felt such a

little time afterwards knowing that her marriage
was nothing but an empty mockery.

It was foolish to ask herself what had brought
this mood on; she knew only too well. If it was
possible to love a man who was virtually a
stranger, and in addition to that was also the
complete antithesis of all that one had ever
wanted in a man, then that was exactly what she
had done where Dominic was concerned.

She loved him. She knew it with a conviction
that was soul-deep, just as she knew that to allow
her love to live was the utmost folly. It was
something that should have been destroyed at
birth, but now it was too late for that.

Trying to shake off her sombre thoughts, she
went inside and made for her bathroom, tugging
off the wet jeans and dropping them on to the
floor as she ran a hot bath.

The hot water and the hard work which should
have soothed her restless nerves and made her
feel tired had no such effect. A restless,
exhausting energy seemed to possess her, tensing
the muscles she was trying to relax. When the
doorbell rang she literally jumped, displacing a
fair quantity of water on to the floor.

She had no idea who might be visiting her at
this time of night, and reached hurriedly for a
towel, wrapping it sarong-wise round her body as
she ran downstairs.

The bell was still ringing, demanding and
imperative, making her fumble with the lock and
then fall back in consternation as the door swung
open and she saw Dominic standing on the step.

Her shock and distress must have been

mirrored on her face, because his own expression changed, his face white and strained in the harsh light from the hall.

Instinctly Kate fell back, groping for the door, shaking as she tried to close it against him.

His foot made it bounce open again, his fingers curling round her wrist, cool against the moist heat of her skin.

'Kate ... no, please ... I have to talk to you.' His voice was low and urgent, and Kate wasn't sure if it was she or he who trembled, only that she could feel the ripples of tension running from where he touched her skin, making her shiver in a fine blending of apprehension and delight. For one crazy moment she actually wanted him to take all responsibility for any decision from her; to force open the door, so that she would be compelled to do whatever it was he wished without actually having to verbally agree to it. Such a thought was so at odds with her normal pattern of behaviour that it numbed her, the sheer force of the feeling he generated inside her leaving her both awed and alarmed.

He saw the fear darkening her eyes and misunderstood the reason for it, saying huskily, 'Kate, don't ... I'm not going to hurt you.'

Incredibly she wanted to laugh. She could feel the beginnings of it welling deep down in her throat and knew that if she did not keep the muscles rigid, it would well out of her in peal after wild peal. Didn't he realise how much he had *already* hurt her? That physical violence from him was the very last thing she feared?

'Let me come inside. I . . . I need to talk to you.'

'Why? To apologise for this afternoon?' She forced herself to sound lightly mocking, avoiding looking directly at him, but even so she was aware of the tension investing his movements, but to her amazement he did not rise to the bait as she had expected, but simply said evenly, 'Yes, for that . . . and other things.'

He shocked her so much that she automatically fell back, allowing him to follow her inside.

He was wearing the same jeans and shirt he had had on at lunch, and her senses minutely detailed the texture of his skin where his short-sleeved open-necked shirt revealed it for her inspection. Black hairs darkened his arms and curled just below the base of his throat. She had a mad urge to reach out and touch them, to see if they felt as vibrantly springy as they looked. The scent of his body was all around her, a combination of heat, cologne and musk. It confused and enthralled her, her heightened senses propelling her into a world where the powers of rational thought were drastically reduced.

She sensed a dramatic change in his reaction to her; the bitter resentment that had come across so strongly to her before was gone and in its place was a blend of humility and shame.

'I mean it, Kate. Sue's told me everything . . . about Ricky . . . about your marriage. God, Kate . . . !'

It was the cry of a tormented soul, and her emotions curled away from it in the same way that her sense of hearing cringed back from the sound of chalk squealing across a blackboard; a refined form of torture which owed nothing to actual physical pain, but which was highly traumatic nonetheless.

As though she was set apart from what was going on she noted that Dominic didn't ask why she had not told him the truth, her control shattered by a welling sadness because they both knew that he would not have believed her; that he would not have wanted to believe her, just as she would have preferred him never to have learned it. It was safer that way—for both of them. Their mutual hostility had been a form of security, protecting them from . . . From what? From love? Kate shuddered then, acknowledging the full force of her feelings for him, and saw as he reached out to touch her that he had misinterpreted her fear as revulsion.

His whole face darkened as a tide of colour swept up under his skin, his eyes naked and vulnerable as they met hers. It was more than she could bear; that she had to carry the burden of his feelings as well as her own, and she pulled away from him with a despairing moan so that his fingers missed her arm and instead grasped the loose edge of her towel.

So it was that fate ordained that which must happen and that which must not, she saw, as she felt the towel slip away from her body and saw Dominic's face contort in a mixture of longing, anguish and pain. A human being could only fight so much . . . or manoeuvre so much.

She didn't move . . . didn't try to run as he

scooped her up in his arms, his muscles contracting with effort, his breathing shallow and tense against her skin.

He carried her to the guest bedroom as she had known he would, laying her down on the bed as though she was a fragile and delicate as the petal of a flower, touching her skin with fingers that trembled convulsively, a blind, despairing look in the eyes that absorbed every detail of her naked body.

In silence he undressed and in silence Kate waited. An odd calm possessed her, a feeling that what was happening was something that was meant to be. She had tried to prevent it; she had tried to protect herself, but at every turn fate had conspired against her, and now there was no point in fighting any further.

Her calm was not one of numb acceptance, but the desire running so strongly within her was not something she yet felt able to express. It was almost as though some inner voice was urging her to wait . . . to channel and control her need. And the moment Dominic lay down beside her and took her in his arms, she knew why.

Sensation after sensation exploded inside her, each one newer and more forceful than the last, and yet she was still able to monitor and register Dominic's need and desire for her.

They made love avidly, feverishly, desperately hungry for one another, with no desire or need for any leisurely preliminaries. They might almost have been lovers of several years' standing, parted and now reunited, so readily did their bodies merge together.

Neither of them spoke; their desire too savage and consuming for words, the thick silence punctuated only by the sounds of their bodies moving urgently together, taking what they had both, in their separate ways, deliberately denied themselves in the past.

Kate felt no gradual build-up to the climax she had read so much about, but never before actually experienced, her body simply exploded in a frenzied burst of sensation that took Dominic's with it. He cried out, the first sound he had made since entering the room, and then as the tumult eased from their bodies and he lay down beside her, taking her into his arms, Kate thought she felt the dampness of his tears against her skin.

Drowsily as sleep claimed her it came to her that her body was at peace, but that for her heart, the pain was only just about to begin.

# CHAPTER SEVEN

SHE woke from a deep sleep during the filtering grey light of the false dawn, to find Dominic watching her, his head supported by his hand, his features indistinct in the poor light, but the tension in his body openly apparent.

'What is it . . .? What's wrong?'

Alarm and apprehension contracted her muscles, memories of the past and his contempt of her overwhelming the delicious languor with which she had woken.

Dominic reached out to touch her, his fingertips tracing the outline of her face, following the curve of her mouth, before suddenly he moved away.

She heard the bedclothes rustle and thought that he was leaving her until he said slowly, 'Nothing . . . nothing at all. You're even more than I'd imagined, Kate,' he added softly. 'For eight years I've carried with me an image of you . . . of how you looked in my bed . . . and for most of those eight years I've hated you and myself because I wanted you.' He reached out again and slid his fingers through her hair, tilting her face so that he could look into her eyes.

'I've been so wrong about you,' he told her rawly, 'Can you forgive me?'

It wasn't a declaration of love or adoration, but it held a ring of genuine remorse that made her ache both for him and for herself.

'I should have realised ... seen ...' he went on.

'How could you have done? I was Ricky's wife.'

'But you're not any more—thank God,' he interrupted her roughly, his voice taking on a yearning quality as he added thickly, 'Kate, I want you so much.'

Instinctively, blindly, she raised her face to his, his fingers sliding down to grip the delicate bones of her shoulders, tension hardening his body as he muttered against her ear, 'I hope you mean this, Kate, because I'm afraid if you don't, it's too late for turning back now. Eight years I've ached for you ... dreamed about you, cursed the day I ever met you. You've become almost an obsession to me, Kate, and now ...'

'And now what?' she asked lightly, suddenly almost afraid of the tension surrounding them both; afraid of placing too much meaning in what he was saying to her.

'And now I'm almost afraid to touch you,' he admitted huskily.

Her apprehension dropped away. Slowly she reached up and touched his mouth with her fingers, drawn to do so by a compulsion that had stalked her for days.

'Don't be,' she whispered as she felt the firm flesh burn beneath her touch, and shivered herself in response.

'Kate!' He said her name on a hoarse note of need, obliterated as he pressed his mouth to the palm of her hand, his tongue slightly rough and totally erotic as it moved against her skin.

From her palm his lips moved up along her arm, sensitising her skin until she felt as though it burned with a million tiny electric impulses.

It seemed to be a lifetime before he reached her mouth to take her feverishly eager response to him. Her arms wound fiercely round his neck, her fingers shaping the hard bones of his skull beneath the silky thickness of his hair.

When his hand cupped her breast she moaned through his kiss, the sound trapped deep in her throat but obviously recognised by him, and his kiss hardened into dark passion in response to the eager stiffening of her nipple beneath his touch.

When his mouth left hers to move down the slimness of her throat she dragged in lungfuls of air, shuddering violently when she felt it against the hardened peak of her breast.

Her body arched against his mouth in longing and in pleasure, her fingers digging into the bunched muscles of his shoulders.

Against her she could feel his arousal, his desire feeding on and fuelling her own, the heat she could feel moving slowly through her veins echoed by the way his skin burned under her touch.

His mouth found her other breast, tugging gently on her swollen nipple until she felt almost faint with the frenzy of feeling he was arousing inside her.

Her desire was as great as it had been last night, but this time he was not rushing their lovemaking, but drawing out the pleasure of it until it stretched like an almost too fine note of music that ravished almost to the point of pain.

Beneath her hands his skin felt like warm satin, fluid and yet firm. She touched his chest tentatively, stopping suddenly as the past caught up with her and she heard Ricky's voice, sharp with dislike as he pushed her away from his body, contemptuous of her hesitantly naïve caresses.

'Kate . . .'

Her eyes focused anxiously on Dominic's, trying to hold their steady regard. 'What is it?'

Her mind jumped, veering sharply away from telling him. She wanted to know the full intimacy of his body, to caress him with her hands and lips, but the past would not release its hold on her. She felt Dominic's glance drop to where her fingers lay curled mutely against his chest, and felt him sigh and knew he was aware of her reluctance to touch him. But he did not know the reason why. She was frightened . . . haunted by the lingering poison left by Ricky's cruelty; and haunted too by the fact that once this man also had rejected her. It was all right as long as he was the one doing the caressing . . . making the running, but though there was desire between them, there was no trust, she thought sadly.

'Kate.'

His eyes burned dark gold in the immobility of his face, his chest rising and falling sharply, his skin flushed and hot. His hand cupped her face, his mouth moving gently against her own, and then far less gently as he felt her eager response. This was something she felt safe with.

His mouth left hers and she watched the dark tide of colour film his cheekbones; felt the hard compression of his muscles as he bent towards her, his chest pressed hard against her breasts.

She could feel the faint edge of violence, just beneath the surface of his passion, and oddly it thrilled her, shocking her into an awareness of just how little she had known about passion—until now. Now she was learning fast . . . too fast, an inner voice warned her, but Dominic's mouth was against her skin, his fingers stroking delicately between her thighs, making her forget everything but the surge of need pounding through her. Her body arched ecstatically against his hand, her strangled sob of pleasure smothered against his skin as she pressed shaking lips to his throat, wantonly responsive in her need to attain the shimmering delight that beckoned her on.

This time he made love to her slowly, teasing her a little with the tormenting, measured thrust of his body into her own, until she cried out in agonised despair, digging her nails into his back and whimpering with a need that made him abandon his role as a controlled lover, to possess her with a fiercely elemental hunger that matched and then exceeded her own. Quivering in the aftermath of the violently climatic convulsions that had gripped her, she could hardly believe it when he continued to move within her, drawing from her an explosion of sensation so intense that for a moment it seemed she actually lost consciousness, his voice as he reached his own release reaching her as though from a far distance.

Even when he had withdrawn from her, her body continued to tremble, slick with sweat

which was now rapidly cooling her skin. She felt
him move and gather her into his arms, too weak
to do anything other than simply lie against him.

Against her ear she felt his lips move, his voice
a deep rumble she could almost feel inside her as
he muttered softly, 'Forgive me, Kate, I've
exhausted you. I hadn't intended to be so . . .
demanding, but eight years is a long time to go
hungry for a woman . . .'

A woman? she thought drowsily, trying to
unravel the error she felt sure was within the
words. Dominic couldn't have meant that there
had been no woman with whom he had made love
in that time . . . No, of course he could not, and
she was a fool for even thinking he might. He had
been speaking metaphorically, that was all. Her
body ached, but it was a pleasant ache, reminding
her that this was the first time she had ever tasted
passion. She wasn't sure, but as she drifted off to
sleep she thought she felt Dominic's mouth
gently caressing her moist skin, trailing a tender
path from her throat to the slight swell of her
belly, before his arms curved round her again and
she finally relaxed into exhaustion.

When she woke up again it was daylight and
Dominic was gone. She stretched in languorous
pleasure, blinking slowly like a large cat before
rolling over to lie in the spot which had held
Dominic's body.

She could smell the scent of him on her skin,
and shivered slightly, uncomfortably conscious of
how little it seemed to take to arouse her body to
the pitch where she was achingly conscious of
how they had made love. Her breasts ached

slightly, her nipples tight and faintly swollen. If Dominic were here beside her now she would want him to make love to her. Swiftly banishing the thought, she pushed back the covers and headed for her bathroom, standing under the cooling lash of the shower while she tried to get a grip on her tumultuous emotions.

Not only did the cool water quench her desire, it also brought her shiveringly back to reality. What had happened last night had been so totally unexpected that it had completely pushed reality aside—for both of them perhaps, but this morning Dominic was gone, which surely indicated very clearly that he considered what had passed between them to be something he certainly did not wish to discuss and perhaps even regretted.

Surely if he had had any genuine feelings for her at all he would have wanted to be with her when she woke up, but he had gone . . . without a word to her.

Slowly drying herself, Kate went back to her bedroom and made herself go over the events of the previous evening. Dominic had been in something almost approaching a state of shock when he arrived. And no doubt it had been a shock to him to learn how wrong he had been about her. That he had learned it gave her no thrill of pleasure—on the contrary, all she could feel was an aching pain that it had taken remorse and guilt to bring him to her. Against her will she remembered how intensely he had wanted her, how fiercely he had made love to her. But desire, no matter how fierce, was not love. Dominic did not love her. How could he? He himself had told

her how much he resented his desire for her, and
now added to that resentment would be the guilt
of knowing how wrongly he had misjudged her.

All the time she was dressing, her actions those
of an automaton, Kate was going over and over
what had happened, and her body shook as she
remembered his passionate desire for her and her
own response to it. She had been so carried away
by their mutual need that nothing else had been
important, but that could not be allowed to
happen again.

Already she was terrified by the knowledge of
how much she yearned for him. It would be far
too dangerous to allow herself to get any further
involved with him.

She would probably not be called upon to
make any such choice, she reminded herself
wryly. After all, Dominic had left without saying
anything about getting in touch with her. No, if
she was sensible she would look upon last night
as something which should have happened eight
years ago; something infinitely precious to her,
but also something that could never be repeated.

Despite her firm resolve several times during
the morning she found her hands growing still
over their tasks, her mind drifting back to the
previous evening, her body languid with remembered pleasure, until reality intruded and
she shuddered back to reality.

It was pointless and self-deluding to allow
herself to be deceived by some romantic fantasy.
Last night Dominic had been a man held in thrall
to the grip of very strong emotions, and man-like
he had exorcised those emotions by the most

physical means possible. No doubt today he was feeling as annoyed with himself for giving in to his desire for her as he had previously been at experiencing that desire. People did not change overnight; it might even be that Dominic resented learning the truth about her.

It was to stop herself thinking about her feelings for him that Kate kept herself so busy trying to second-guess Dominic's emotions and thoughts, she thought wryly as she finally abandoned her half-hearted attempt to work. For once not even the prospect of starting on a new commission had the power to thrill her. A tiny shiver of sensation rippled over her skin. No, it seemed that Dominic alone now had that power. Angry with herself, she forced back the thought. It was pointless to build crazy dreams on what her intellect told her were the most flimsy of foundations. It would be reckless folly indeed to invite even more pain by allowing herself to believe that she meant something to Dominic as a person.

Round and round her thoughts chased one another, exhausting her mentally, but leaving her physically strained and on edge.

When she heard a car coming up the drive her first thought was that it must be Dominic, and she flew to the window, fighting down a crashing sense of disappointment when she recognised Vera getting out of her husband's car.

Forcing a smile to her lips, she opened the door to her.

'Hi . . . I hope I'm not interrupting your work, but I'm at a bit of a loose end. Ian and Dominic have gone to the City for some business discussions, so I thought I'd come round and see you.' She gazed appreciatively around the hall. 'This is really lovely, Kate, you must be very sad at the thought of parting with it.'

'In some ways, yes,' Kate agreed. 'But it was Ricky's family home and . . .'

'Of course, how tactless of me!' Vera looked mortified. 'Of course, you can't enjoy living somewhere that reminds you——'

'No . . . no . . . it isn't like that at all,' Kate assured her. 'As a matter of fact, I always think of it as being Ricky's grandfather's house. I used to come over here a lot with my father when he was alive. It is lovely, but I just can't afford to keep it in the style to which it's become accustomed,' she joked ruefully.

She was aching to ask Vera when Dominic was coming back, but even as she tried to think of a casual enough way to frame her question her tongue seemed to stick to the roof of her mouth. What a ridiculous way for a woman of twenty-seven to behave, she chastised herself, especially when she had just spent all morning reminding herself that there was no future for her with Dominic . . . no basis between them for any sort of continuing relationship at all. It was high time she faced the truth, unpalatable though it might be. As far as Dominic was concerned, she was just a woman he had needed to get out of his system in the most primitive way possible, and now that that had been achieved . . . Witness the way he had not even bothered to wait for her to wake up this morning . . . had not even left her a note, or bothered to get in touch with her.

She showed Vera over the house and then the gardens, listening with half an ear while the other woman marvelled admiringly at them.

Once they were back inside Kate offered her tea, and they sat drinking it together in the drawing-room, Kate's thoughts wandering painfully back to Dominic, so that she didn't realise that Vera had gone quiet until the latter said abruptly, 'It's such a pity that you and Dominic don't hit it off, you . . .'

Dreading what Vera might be about to say, Kate interrupted hastily, 'Oh, it isn't really important—after all, we're not likely to ever seem that much of one another.'

The phone rang, shocking her into silence. She stared at it helplessly for several seconds before she realised that Vera was watching her with a rather puzzled frown. Tense with longing and dread, she walked over to it and picked up the receiver, an intense feeling of disappointment attacking her as she recognised Martin Allwood's voice.

'Hope I'm not disturbing you,' he began, unconsciously echoing Vera's words on her arrival. 'But we've got the printed detail sheet for the house back now, and I wondered if I could pop round later to show it to you.'

She ached to say no, to blot out anything that would stop her from re-living over and over again the previous night, but she forced herself to fight down the impulse, saying instead, 'Yes, of course, I'd like that.'

'The thing is it will have to be this evening, say about nine-ish? I've got to call and view a house at eight, so with a bit of luck I could call on you on the way back.'

Agreeing to his suggestion, Kate replaced the receiver. Vera was watching her with unabashed interest.

'Just the estate agent,' she told her, wondering why on earth she sounded so defensive.

Vera grinned. 'So I gathered. Sue thinks he's fallen for you.'

'Sue's a committed romantic,' retorted Kate, grimacing faintly. 'She's been trying to get me married off for the best part of the last six years.'

'But you've obviously never been tempted?' Vera looked openly curious, and Kate felt her heart contract in pain. She had no wish to offend Vera, but there was simply no way that she could confide in her. Without realising it her eyes had darkened with pain, betraying something of her feelings.

'Forgive me, Kate,' Vera said gently, 'I'm prying and I shouldn't. It's one of my worst traits, but I'm afraid that like Sue, I'm a hopeless romantic too. Mind you, I'm often way, way off target.' She made a rueful moue and said lightly, 'You won't believe this, but the first time I saw you and Dominic together, I couldn't help but think what an attractive couple you made.'

Kate disguised her sharp gasp of anguish by bending down as though she had knocked herself against the telephone table. Fortunately she had been able to turn her face away from Vera's, and the other woman was still chattering blithely to her, thankfully oblivious to her traitorous response to the sound of Dominic's name.

It was just gone five o'clock when Vera left, explaining that she had promised to pick Ian up from the station. Which must mean that Dominic was not returning to the village, Kate thought painfully.

She told herself that she ought to be pleased ... relieved that she was not going to be obliged to see him. It was far better that there should be a clean break like this, rather than the torture of a fully fledged affair, ending when Dominic ultimately tired of her. Yes, she was lucky that his desire for her had been quenched so swiftly, otherwise she might tonight be finding herself in the position of having to lie to him and pretend that she did not want him.

Instinctively she knew it would be very hard to swerve him from a path once he had set his foot upon it, and feeling about him as she did, she doubted that she would have the strength of will to send him away, should he have decided that one night with her was not enough.

And yet the longer she allowed herself to be involved with him, the more helplessly she would become enmeshed in the web of her own feelings for him.

She was a little surprised that she had heard nothing from Sue, she reflected wryly. Her friend must surely be curious to know what effect her revelations had had on him. Unless, of course, Sue was deliberately keeping a low profile, anticipating her anger at being betrayed.

She was just pondering over this when the

phone rang. As soon as she registered Sue's cautious, 'Hi . . .' Kate wondered if there could possibly be such a thing as E.S.P.

They chatted for a few minutes, neither of them mentioning Dominic. Kate felt as though her nerves were being stretched on fine wires and that they now just needed the merest touch to snap them completely.

When Sue eventually mentioned Dominic, she froze, thankful that her friend could not see her face.

'I'm afraid I lost my temper with him yesterday,' Sue confessed. 'And what's worse, I blurted out to him the truth about your marriage to Ricky. I don't know which of us was the more shocked! You know what I'm like when my temper explodes. I don't suppose you've seen anything of him?'

If she told Sue that Dominic had been round to see her, her friend would want to know what had happened. She knew Sue of old, she would not rest until she had prised every last detail from her, and that was something she could not bear, no matter how well-meant Sue's curiosity might be, so instead of telling the truth she lied, squashing the feelings of guilt stirring uncomfortably inside her.

'Ought I to have done?' she asked lightly. The receiver slid stickily in her hand, tension making her shake.

'Maybe not . . . It's just that I thought he might have hot-footed it round to your place to apologise. It certainly gave him one hell of a jolt.'

'I expect it did. No one likes having their

judgment proved wrong, but it was all over a long time ago, Sue.'

'Not for you it wasn't,' Sue contradicted her. 'His rejection of you left painful scars, Kate, we both know that. I . . . Oh damn,' she cursed, 'someone's just come to the door. I'll try to come over and see you tomorrow, Kate. Must go now . . . 'Bye!'

Grateful to whoever Sue's visitor was for her reprieve, Kate replaced the receiver and wandered back into the study. She had hardly touched her work today. Damn Dominic! She didn't want him intruding in her life, in her thoughts in this far too pervasive way.

She worked for close on an hour knowing, when she had finished, that most of what she had done was completely worthless, and neither had she been remotely successful in banishing Dominic from her thoughts.

The sound of a car outside made her glance at her watch and frown. It was a quarter to nine. Martin Allwood was early. She got up and hurried into the hall, opening the door at his first ring, but the pleasant smile she had forced on to her face faded as she saw not Martin Allwood, but Dominic standing outside.

He was in the hall before she could even think of closing the door on him, the dark business suit and contrasting white shirt he was wearing immediately reminding her of the very first time she had seen him.

He looked tired, she noted painfully, his mouth drawn tight in uncompromising anger as he demanded harshly,

'Why did you lie to Sue about not seeing me?'

His question was so totally unexpected that it threw her completely, leaving her to stare at him while her brain tried to come up with a satisfactory response.

'Are you so ashamed of making love with me that my presence here last night is something that has to be lied about and hidden? It's okay to make love with me, but only as long as no one else knows about it, is that it?'

Kate struggled to understand the reason for his bitterness. Surely that was *her* line? After all, he was the one who had disappeared without a word or a note. But instead of challenging him with this all she could do was to stammer nervously, 'How do you know what I said to Sue?'

'Because I arrived at her house just after she had finished speaking to you. I went round there to apologise for my previous manner towards her, and she was rather surprised that I had taken the time and trouble to apologise to her, but not to you.' He saw her expression and his mouth twisted in a bitter smile. 'Oh, don't worry,' he told her harshly, 'I haven't betrayed you.'

Listening to the condemnation in his voice, Kate realised wearily that nothing had changed between them. She had been right to fear any further contact with him. He was still hurting her . . . causing her pain.

She looked at him, intending to ask him to leave, and her whole body trembled. Even without closing her eyes she could picture him as

he had been last night when he made love to
her . . .

'Kate.' His voice had softened to something
almost approaching pleading, and if she hadn't
known better she could almost have sworn there
was pain in his eyes too. 'We have to talk . . .
about last night . . .'

Panic flared inside her. He was going to tell her
that it had all been a mistake, she could feel him
gathering himself together to say so.

'No . . . no . . . there's nothing for us to talk
about,' she interrupted shakily, focusing her eyes
on a point to the right of his shoulder so that she
would not have to look at him. 'We were both a
little carried away by . . . by circumstances . . .
but nothing's really changed, Dominic. We both
know that.'

She had herself under control enough to look at
him now. Instead of looking relieved as she had
expected, he looked bitterly furious, his mouth
compressed in a hard line as he flung at her,

'You want me!'

Oh, the humiliation of it . . . of him standing
there and stating so trenchantly the obviousness
of her desire for him. She searched feverishly for
some means of defence that would not involve
her in an outright lie, and managed huskily,

'I wanted you eight years ago as well, but
wanting isn't loving, Dominic.'

For a moment there was silence and then he
asked harshly, 'Have I asked you for love?'

Her skin whitened under the taunt, and she
knew then that she had been right to be wary of
seeing him again. The pain was now worse, far

worse than it had been before, because now he
knew so much more about her; could hurt her in
so many more ways.

There was nothing more she could say. By
coming here and saying to her what he had
Dominic had confirmed all her own worse doubts
and fears about their relationship. Relationship?
What relationship? she mocked herself savagely.
She had simply been a one-night stand; a means
of appeasing a physical hunger which she had
known he deeply resented.

She walked to the door suddenly feeling very,
very old, and opened it, turning to look blindly at
him.

'I think you'd better leave, Dominic.'

'If that's what you want.' He sounded
completely indifferent, almost callously so.

He was just about to leave when Martin
Allwood's car came up the drive. Kate kept her
eyes fixed on it, but still she felt Dominic turn to
look at her, his glance almost seeming to burn her
sensitive skin.

'So that's it,' he said curtly. 'He can't be very
good in bed, Kate,' he added coolly as he stepped
through the door. 'Otherwise, you'd never have
responded to me the way you did last night. He's
very like Rick, isn't he? Take care, Kate. It's
criminal folly to make the same mistake twice.'

He was gone before she could retort, nodding
abruptly to Martin as the latter climbed out of his
car.

'Odd sort of chap,' commented Martin, as Kate
showed him into the house. 'For some reason I
get the feeling he doesn't much care for me.

Good friend of yours, is he?' he asked Kate speculatively as she closed the door.

'He was a friend of my husband's,' Kate told him repressively. She suspected that Martin was something of a gossip and she did not want him gossiping about Dominic and herself, especially not now . . .

What had he wanted to talk to her about? she wondered as she took Martin into the drawing-room and offered him a drink, her movements when he accepted automatic, her mind totally engrossed by the purpose of Dominic's visit.

He had wanted to make his position clear to her, that was all, she derided herself. He had wanted to make sure that she understood that there was no real significance about what had happened last night. No doubt he had been anxious that she should not get the wrong idea . . . not make demands upon him or assumptions about the future.

Well, he need not have bothered. She knew exactly what the situation was.

Abruptly she became aware that Martin had stopped talking. Flushing slightly, she looked at him to find that he was eyeing her with frowning curiosity.

'I'm sorry,' she apologised, 'I was thinking about my work.'

'I was just asking you what you thought of the leaflet.'

He was holding it in his hand and Kate took it from him, forcing herself to concentrate her attention on it.

It was gone ten o'clock when he eventually left.

He had been disposed to stay and chat, and eventually she had been forced to make an outright claim to being tired to get him to go.

At the front door he had paused to ask her out for dinner, but Kate had refused. She was too exhausted emotionally to even think of going out with anyone else.

# CHAPTER EIGHT

TRYING to appear normal in front of Sue when she arrived the following afternoon was one of the hardest things Kate had ever had to do. Sue was obviously eager to regale her with all the details of the scene between Dominic and herself, but Kate forestalled her, causing her to frown slightly.

'Kate, surely you don't still feel so strongly about him that you can't even bear to hear his name mentioned?'

She did, but not in the way that Sue meant.

'It's not that,' she lied, 'it's just that I've got so much on my mind already, what with this commission from Vera and Ian, and then selling the house.'

'Of course.' Sue's ready sympathy only increased her sense of guilt. 'You must be feeling really down about having to part with this place. Has anyone been round to view it yet?'

'No.'

Having been distracted away from the subject of Dominic, Sue continued to chat blithely for another half an hour before announcing that she had to go to collect the children from school.

'You need a holiday, Kate,' she chided her friend as she left. 'You're looking far too tired. You need to get away.'

Sue was right, Kate reflected when her friend

had gone. She did need to get away—from
Dominic. Perhaps if she went to stay with Harry
and Liz for a few days? She had a standing
invitation to visit them . . .

She would see how she felt tomorrow, she told
herself as she walked out into the garden. Some
weeding might help to take her mind off
Dominic. She was still outside when the phone
rang.

It was the receptionist from the estate agent's
office calling to ask if it would be convenient to
send someone round to view the property that
afternoon.

'Unfortunately all the partners have appoint-
ments,' she told Kate. 'Would you be able to
show the people round yourself?'

Confirming that she would, Kate made a note
of the time they were expected and replaced the
receiver.

It was just after half-past two when Kate heard
the doorbell. She was in the kitchen, arranging
some flowers she had brought in from the garden,
and she wiped her hands on a towel before
hurrying to the door, cursing herself as she
realised she had neglected to ask the receptionist
the name of the prospective purchasers.

She opened the door with what she hoped was
a cool smile, her facial muscles stiffening as she
saw Dominic standing outside.

'I told you I didn't want to see you again!' The
words sounded more like a cry of anguish than the
cold remonstrance she had intended them to be.

Mouth grim, Dominic stepped past her, cold
topaz eyes meeting her own with derisory

mockery as he told her, 'It isn't you I've come to see. It's the house.'

It took a few seconds for his meaning to seep in. Mouth agape, Kate stared at him.

'You mean you've come to view the house?'

'Full marks, you've got it in one.'

The taunt was cold and hostile, but Kate ignored it as anger boiled up inside her.

'I don't know what you think you're doing, Dominic,' she raged at him. 'But if you think that by pretending you want to buy this house——'

'Who says I'm pretending?' He had been studying the gallery and swung round now, to look at her coolly. 'I need a base in England now that I'm going into partnership with Ian, and where better to live than in the same locality?' His mouth twisted and he added softly, 'Or were you flattering yourself that the house was just a pretext—an excuse to come and see you?'

Her face burned with humiliated embarrassment, her voice and movements stiff as she ignored his question to ask curtly instead, 'Where would you like to start? Upstairs or down?'

'Oh, down, I think,' he said softly. 'Then we can finish up upstairs.'

There was nothing in his eyes other than a certain flat hardness, but Kate was convinced she had not imagined the taunting hint of sexual innuendo behind his words. He was deliberately trying to ruffle her, she realised. No doubt his pride was suffering because she had been the first to say that there was no future for them. Obviously he had wanted to be the one to say that to her.

She showed him round the ground floor of the house, gritting her teeth every time she felt him brush past her, or stand close to her. She was so sensitive to him that it almost hurt to breathe. She wanted to hate and resent him, but her weak, traitorous body yearned for him to hold and caress it.

He followed her upstairs, waiting while she opened each bedroom door, a malicious smile darkening his eyes as she stood on one side on the landing in an attitude of frozen rigidity.

'Not going to come in with me, Kate?' he asked, when he walked into the room where they had made love. 'Why not, I wonder? Are you frightened that——'

It was too much for her. Trembling violently, she interrupted him, 'I'm not in the least frightened of you, Dominic!'

He turned his head and she caught the glint of pure mockery in his eyes as he drawled, 'Of course not, I never thought for one moment that you were. Why should you be? You shouldn't anticipate, Kate. What I was going to say was, are you perhaps frightened of what being in this bedroom with me might do to that icy self-control you've wrapped yourself in?'

Some instinct for self-protection made her retaliate sharply, her body tensing as she said coolly, 'Now *you're* leaping to conclusions, Dominic.'

He swung round, pinning her with narrowed eyes. Fear touched her like someone touching an exposed nerve, making her jump and then start shaking inwardly.

'Meaning?' he demanded softly.

She couldn't speak. Her tongue seemed to be stuck to the roof of her mouth. He was coming towards her, advancing with almost menacing intent, and although she longed to turn and run she simply could not move.

'Kate?'

The total unexpectedness of Martin Allwood's voice in the hall below shocked her out of her fear. Both she and Dominic stared towards the stairs. They had been so engrossed in their mutual battling that neither of them had heard him arrive.

'So . . .' She saw Dominic's eyes harden and flinched beneath the contempt in them. 'He won't make you happy, Kate,' he told her harshly. 'He simply isn't man enough for you.'

'While you, I suppose, are!' she managed to hiss back in a furious whisper as Martin came upstairs.

'My secretary told me she'd sent someone round to see the house.' He did a double-take as he saw Dominic, and then frowned.

'Kate has just about finished showing me round,' Dominic told him smoothly, instantly regaining control of himself, the savagery he had shown her completely gone, Kate noted shakenly. His glance encompassed them both, but it was Martin he spoke to as he said urbanely, 'I'm very interested in the property, but perhaps we might discuss it in your office, Allwood.'

The miraculous speed with which Martin's manner towards him changed totally amazed Kate. Before she knew what was happening

both Dominic and Martin were leaving—
together.

It wasn't because Dominic had gone that she
felt so bereft, Kate told herself forlornly as she
went back to the kitchen and her flowers. It was
simply ... With a brief gesture of disgust she
pushed the flowers away. What was the point of
lying to herself? She loved him, she knew she did,
and that was why she had been fighting so hard
against any involvement with him. But she was
already involved on the very deepest level that
there was. She shivered suddenly, rubbing the
gooseflesh prickling her arms. What did it matter
how she felt about Dominic, he cared nothing for
her?

Was he serious about buying the house? She
thought about how she would feel having him as
her closest neighbour, and her whole body shook.
Suddenly she had to get out of the house, to
escape from the place where she had been most
intimate with him.

She would go down to the cottage; that held no
memories of Dominic at all. She had made a start
on cleaning it, but there was still a lot left to do.

She worked well into the evening, giving the
largest bedroom, which she had decided would be
her own, a thorough cleaning. The old-fashioned
high mahogany bed which had been her grand-
parents' she rather liked and had decided to keep.
The room faced north, and was decorated in a
depressing browny-orange. When she had
finished cleaning the paintwork Kate sat back on
her heels and studied it, mentally substituting the
old-fashioned wallpaper with something more in

keeping ... something traditional, perhaps tiny
pink rosebuds on a white background. She could
have a soft pink carpet and heavily starched old-
fashioned white cotton bedlinen lavishly trimmed
with lace. There was a rocking chair in one of the
rooms that could be re-polished. She had already
stripped the bed on her previous visit, and now
on an impulse she hurried into one of the other
rooms where a bedding chest contained the
bedlinen which had once been her grandmother's.
Her father had been the type of person who never
threw anything out. One of her mother's many
grievances about him had been that he forced her
to live with his parents' old-fashioned cast-off
furniture, but now it, and the linen that went
with it, was coming back into fashion again.

Amazingly as Kate opened the chest the scent
of lavender filled the air, and she wondered wryly
if her father had actually ever opened the chest.
She took out clean white sheets and carried them
into the other room, spreading one on the bed
and then standing back to judge the effect, but it
was impossible to gain an impression of exactly
how the room would look redecorated. It was a
large bed, meant to hold two people, not one, and
unnervingly as she stared at it, she could almost
see Dominic's lean tanned body tangled in the
white sheets, his dark head on the pillow.

Stop it ... stop it! she warned herself angrily,
tensing as she heard a car. She went to the
window, stunned to see Dominic getting out of
the parked BMW.

For a moment she was almost tempted to hide
... to pretend that she was not there. She

frowned ... How had he known where to find her ... and more important, why had he *wanted* to find her?

By the time she had got downstairs she thought she had come up with the answer. Opening the door to him, she said curtly, 'If it's about the house, then please discuss it with my estate agent ...'

She was about to close the door again when he wrested it from her and stepped determinedly inside.

'It isn't about the house,' he told her bluntly.

For a moment a wild hope flared inside her, but there was nothing even remotely lover-like in the way he was looking at her. Quenching her disappointment, she looked at him.

'What are you doing here, then?'

'I've come to warn you that two men have broken out of the high security prison. It was on the news when I was in the car. I went to your place and found you gone ... then as I was driving past, I saw your car parked here.'

'Two men ...' Kate's forehead creased in a frown. It was of course a very serious matter, but hardly important enough for him to have delivered the news in person.

'The police don't think they've gone very far. In fact they suspect they're probably keeping under cover at the moment—they're both armed, but they're still in prison uniform. The first thing they're going to want is a change of clothes, food, money, and possibly some form of security.'

'Security ...?' Kate was baffled until Dominic exclaimed harshly, 'Hostages, Kate ... bargaining counters so that the police are forced to let them go free.'

'Hostages ... You mean ...?' She looked at him and read the truth in his grim face. 'You think they might ...?' Her voice tailed away faintly as she remembered how close the cottage and her house were to the prison, and how remote from anything else, and she shivered slightly. 'I ...'

'You're coming back to the house with me, now,' Dominic told her curtly, 'and I'm staying the night. And before you start making any objections, my motives are entirely altruistic. Tomorrow we'll make other arrangements. You can stay with Vera and Ian, or your friend Sue, but it's too late for any of that tonight.' He glanced at his watch. 'It's gone ten now. In another half an hour it will be dark.'

Kate shivered beneath the grimness of his voice, her mind conjuring up unpleasant pictures of the loneliness of the landscape around the cottage.

'Nothing to say?'

Her mouth had gone dry and she touched her lips tentatively with the tip of her tongue.

'I'm very grateful to you for your concern,' she said woodenly at last, 'but ...'

'Well, you are the widow of an old friend,' Dominic said derisively. 'Oh, it's all right, Kate,' he added curtly, completely misreading the haunted expression that crossed her face, 'I've no intention of usurping Allwood's role in your life.' His mouth curled a little as he asked her tauntingly, 'Does he know yet that you and I have been lovers?'

This was getting ridiculously out of hand. She ought to tell Dominic that Martin Allwood meant absolutely nothing to her, but somehow she could not.

'Aren't you frightened *I* might not be able to resist the temptation to tell him?' he demanded savagely, watching her recoil from the cruelty of his words with something almost approaching pleasure.

Kate felt as though she was being torn apart. Why was he torturing her like this?

'Why ... why should you do that?' she managed unevenly at last.

'Why?' He looked both incredulous and furious. He moved and for one moment Kate thought he actually meant to shake her, then he stepped back again, cursing softly under his breath.

'Let's get out of here,' he told her flatly, propelling her towards the door with a hand on the flat of her back.

Kate let him move her, protesting only when she reached her car that she could not leave it there and travel back with him. He let her get in it and waited for her to start it up, following her all the way back to the house, and parking his BMW next to her Mini so that she was blocked in.

Although she didn't want him staying with her, he was right about it being too late for her to foist herself off on either Vera or Sue tonight, and she certainly did not relish the prospect of being alone in the house with two dangerous criminals on the loose.

Dominic followed her inside the house, carefully locking the door behind him. It had bolts as well as a lock, although Kate rarely used them. It gave her a strange feeling as she watched Dominic slide them into place, almost as though suddenly they were separated from the rest of the world.

'I'll go round and check all the windows and doors.'

Kate made a small sound of protest in her throat and watched him turn to look at her. As he stood in the shadows his face took on a closed, almost remote, look as though he was suffering from intense pain.

'Surely that isn't necessary?' she began, only to fall silent when he said quietly, 'You read the papers, don't you, Kate? You must surely remember what happened the other summer?'

Her mind prodded by his words suddenly flung up memories of the dreadful ordeals endured by the inhabitants of a small village which had been terrorised by an escaped gunman. Several women had been raped and . . . Kate shuddered, and Dominic said quietly, 'Yes . . . exactly.'

'I . . . I'll go and make us something to eat,' she offered uncertainly. 'Have you . . . are you . . .?'

'No, I haven't eaten, and yes, I am hungry,' Dominic told her, but Kate had the impression that he knew how desperately she wanted to get her mind off what she had just remembered and that he was saying he was hungry more for her sake than his own. But why should he show her such compassionate caring? It was completely foreign to his nature—at least where she was concerned. She had seen him being charming enough to other people.

Luckily the house insurers had insisted the previous year that Kate have window locks fitted, and while Dominic went round checking that all these were in place and securing them Kate busied herself in the kitchen.

She was acutely conscious of the silence outside in a way that she had never been before, jumping at every tiny sound, the hairs prickling nervously at the back of her neck as she tried to concentrate on making them a simple supper.

The phone rang, but before she could get to it it stopped. Frowning, she went into the drawing-room, to discover Dominic just replacing the receiver.

'That was Sue,' he told her laconically. 'She was worried about you, but I told her I was staying here.'

Kate could feel the colour rising up under her skin. What on earth must Sue be thinking?

'We are living in the twentieth century, you know,' he drawled, watching her. 'It's quite permissible for a woman to have a lover.'

'You're not my lover!' Kate said it more violently than she had intended, her eyes widening as the amusement left his face to be replaced by anger.

'But I have been,' he reminded her softly. 'What is it that frightens you so much that you can't admit the pleasure we gave one another, Kate?' he asked her soberly, reaching out to hold her lightly, his fingers encircling her wrists.

This complete change of tack bemused her, and her eyes lifted to his, her breath coming sharply as she recognised the glitter in his. He still wanted her. Instinctively she moved towards him, checking suddenly. What was she doing?

Quickly she pulled away from him, muttering that she had to make the supper. He let her go, but Kate was conscious of him watching her and her body shook so much she could hardly stand up.

She made them both an omelette and served it with a crisp salad, but it seemed neither of them had much appetite. She watched Dominic covertly while pushing her food round her plate. He was making a pretence of eating, but he was no more enthusiastic than she was herself.

'I'd better ring Vera,' he said abruptly at last. 'I told her I was coming over here and that I intended to stay the night, but I'd better just confirm it.'

While he made his call Kate cleared away their plates and started to make some coffee, which she carried through into the drawing-room. Dominic was standing in the middle of the room, frowning as he listened to a news bulletin on the television.

Kate froze as she heard their village mentioned.

'The police are warning everyone to stay inside,' he told her unnecessarily when the bulletin was over. 'It seems the men are armed and they don't want any members of the public taking chances.'

She shivered, folding her arms protectively around her body. How would she be feeling now if Dominic was not with her? She would have returned from the cottage totally unprepared for the news bulletin, and although she would not have described herself as particularly nervous, even with Dominic here she was having great difficulty in suppressing her memories of the newspaper reports of the incident Dominic had referred to earlier.

'Cold?'

She watched Dominic frown and shook her head, admitting huskily, 'No—scared, but not half as much as I would be if you weren't here.'

Dominic raised his head and looked at her, his gold eyes suddenly gleaming.

'Do you realise that's the first compliment you've ever paid me?' he asked silkily.

He was still watching her, his eyes narrowed, his face a mask of tension.

Inside her something kicked sharply to life, an intense pulsing heat burning through her body. He was wrong. She had already complimented him in the most intimate way possible in abandoning herself to his lovemaking. He was watching her face and she felt as though her thoughts had suddenly become printed on her forehead for him to read. She saw his eyes glitter as he studied the slow crawl of colour up over her skin, his mouth stretching tightly into a mockery of a smile as he asked,

'Now what are you thinking?'

'Not about you!'

It was a childish and dangerous denial, as foolish as the instinctive fear that made her turn and run towards the door. The drawing-room was a comfortable size, but with Dominic in it

with her the air inside the room had suddenly
become impossible to breathe.

He caught her by the door, turning her and
slamming her hard against his body, his face a
mask of sexual excitement and anger.

'You're lying to me, Kate. You were thinking
about me ... about this!' he told her fiercely,
claiming her mouth before she could speak,
thrusting his fingers into her hair and clamping
her head so that she could not avoid the
punishing, drugging force of his kisses.

When she refused to open her mouth he tugged
painfully on her hair, making ruthless use of her
sharp cry of protest.

He was like a man possessed, she thought
feverishly, unstoppable, determined to take what
he wanted with or without her consent. She
should have hated and despised him, but she
didn't. Her body was shaking against his, but not
with shock. The fierce intensity of her answering
desire totally engulfed her. She wanted to be here
like this with him for ever, her mouth dominated
by the hunger of his, all her senses alive. He
leaned further into her and she shuddered as she
felt the intimate contact of his body against her
own.

He moved slightly, and she moaned primitively
deep in her throat, frustration shimmering in her
eyes as she was robbed of the contact with his
body, her head moving tormentedly from side to
side as his mouth lifted from hers, leaving her
bereft.

'Shush ... shush ... It's all right.'

The thick whisper was meant to comfort, but it

only aroused her more, and her flesh quivered in mute pleasure as his hand found her breast.

'Kate . . . Kate, you don't know what you do to me.'

She could hear the tension and excitement in his voice and mindlessly she responded to it.

Where she had been cold now she was burning . . . on fire with the need to have the satin firmness of his flesh against her own without the hindrance of clothes.

She heard him curse as his fingers fumbled with the buttons of her shirt, expelling her breath in an aching sigh of pleasure as he finally cupped the bare skin of her breast. His hips moved against her, his mouth hot and shaking slightly as it touched her throat. The ache of need inside her was something totally outside any previous experience she had had.

Instead of quenching her desire for him the fact that they had already been lovers had only increased it. This was what she had dreaded all along; this terrible searing imprisonment not only of her heart, but also of her body.

His head bent, and she gave a tiny sharp cry of pleasure as she felt his teeth graze delicately over her breast. She was consumed by heat and need; both of which he shared. She could see it in the topaz eyes as she looked down to where his head lay against her breast, his mouth hot against her aching flesh.

A terrible sense of desolation spilled its bitterness inside her.

'Kate . . . I want you . . .'

She heard the words and her heart went cold.

She shook like someone held in the grip of a
fever. Numbly she dragged herself away from
him, inching along the door.

'Kate?'

She caught the edge of violence in his voice, as
he suddenly realised what she was doing.

'What the hell are you trying to do to me,
damn you?' His voice shook, his face a bitter
mask. 'Is that what turns you on? Building me up
and then dropping me flat?'

Kate couldn't speak. She watched him study
her in silence, and then with a tinge of colour
creeping up under his skin he said flatly, 'You're
doing this to punish me, aren't you . . .? *Aren't
you*, damn you?'

His hands were closed, the heat coming off his
body undermining her defences. She could sense
the violence in him and knew that somehow she
must dissipate it. Now without him touching her
she was starting to function normally again. She
was bitterly ashamed of the way she had
responded to him. He had every reason to be
annoyed.

'No . . . No, I wasn't trying to punish you,' she
said slowly at last. Dominic had turned his head
away as though in repudiation of her words, and
impulsively she reached out to touch him,
blenching as he turned his head and looked
wordlessly at where her fingers lay against his
arm.

'Don't do that unless you want us back where
we were ten minutes ago, Kate,' he warned her
expressionlessly. And then withdrawing completely from her he pushed his fingers through

his hair. 'God, what is it about you that brings
out the worst in me? And what is it about me that
makes you deny the physical desire you feel for
me?'

Kate took a deep breath.

'If I deny it, it's because I don't trust it,
Dominic. After all, you want me, but at the same
time you resent that wanting . . . you resent me.'

'Kate, you're wrong.'

She shook her head. 'No . . . Vera's told me
about your mother . . . about your upbringing.'
She avoided his eyes as she said calmly, 'Right
from the first you despised me, Dominic . . . I
think you wanted to despise me. You've told me
yourself that you resented wanting me. I'm still
the same person I was before . . . I haven't
changed.' She was finding it difficult to articulate
her thoughts, but amazingly he seemed to
understand.

'You mean you can't trust a desire that's based
on resentment . . . that you think at some point, if
there was any relationship between us I would
revert to character and turn against you?'

'Yes.'

She heard him sigh. 'Listen to me, Kate,' he
said quietly. 'What Vera told you about my
childhood was true, but with one amendment.
Since the first time you and I met, I've been in
touch with my mother.' He saw her surprise and
smiled bleakly. 'I didn't want to . . . not at first,
but once I did, I was glad. You see, from her I
got a different view of the story; my mother is a
very loving, warm person, unlike my father who
was basically extremely cold. She tried to make

the marriage work, but it was no good.
Eventually after a nervous breakdown her doctor
advised her to get a divorce. My father would
only agree if she allowed me to stay with him.
She didn't want to, but her lawyers advised her
that with her mental history of a breakdown, and
my father's wealth, she would not stand any
chance of being allowed to keep me.

'It's true that the first time we met I did want
to believe the worst of you ... not so much
because of my upbringing, but because I was so
appalled to discover how much I wanted you ...
the wife of a friend. It shook to the foundations
all I had believed about myself; and brought on
the identity crisis that eventually took me in
search of my mother. Kate ...'

He made an appealing gesture towards her, but
she shook her head and shrank back. She didn't
want to hear any more. She wanted to keep as
many barriers between them as possible. That
was the only way she could stay safe. Dominic
wanted her merely on a physical level, but she
loved him.

'Kate ...' he was frowning now, concerned by
her lack of response, and she rushed wildly into
speech to protect herself.

'Dominic, I'm tired ... I'd like to go to bed
... I ...'

She saw the disappointment in his eyes and it
convulsed her with remorse. Something almost
approaching pain shadowed them and she longed
to go to him and take him in her arms, but she
could not afford to be weak. She had far too
much to lose.

'Very well.' His face looked strained, his smile forced. 'I had hoped we might talk, but if you're tired . . .'

'It's been a long day.'

'Yes.'

He turned his back and walked over to the fire, and ridiculously Kate found herself wanting to linger . . . torn between common sense and desire. If he turned round and looked at her the choice would be made for her, and she trembled, waiting . . . but he did not. Quietly she opened the door and slid through it, telling herself that she had made the wisest choice.

# CHAPTER NINE

SOMETHING was pressing down on her, stifling her, threatening to deprive her of breath.

Kate came awake with a jolt. Her heart was pounding violently, her breathing erratic. She had been having a nightmare. She shivered, suddenly cold where she had been hot, and then froze as her ears picked up an alien sound. Sitting tensely in her bed, hands clasped round her knees, she listened, hardly daring to breathe.

Yes ... that had definitely been the kitchen door to the hall opening, she would recognise its squeak anywhere.

Terror galvanised her into action, taking her out of bed and towards her door before she even had time to think properly. The landing was in darkness, of course, but she knew it so well she did not need any light. Her pulse was drumming against her skin, fear releasing adrenalin into her blood.

Someone had broken into the house. She had to tell Dominic—that was the thought that was uppermost in her mind as she stood poised by her open door, judging the distance to Dominic's room, trying to remember if there were any boards likely to creak. The air she breathed seemed heavy and thick with tension, her lungs expanding only with difficulty. God, she was so frightened! As she moved out on to the landing it crossed her mind to

wonder at what her fear would have been if she had
been alone in the house.

She was halfway there when something made
her tense and turn to look back towards the stairs.
The fine hairs lining her skin prickled upwards in
atavistic terror as she saw the dark, bulky shape
coming slowly towards her.

For a moment she was too shocked to do
anything, and then her paralysis broke, a sharp
scream tearing the muscles of her throat as she
realised the intruder had seen her and was
coming towards her, reaching out to her.

A black void opened up beneath her and she
felt herself falling dizzily into it. In the distance
someone called her name, the voice deep and
familiar. She struggled to respond, but the
darkness whirled faster and faster around her,
sucking her down with a noise like a train going
through a tunnel.

'Kate?'

Behind her closed eyelids patterns broke and
re-formed. She frowned, recognising the voice,
but knowing that its urgent note of concern was
alien to her knowledge of it. She wanted to open
her eyes, but her eyelids felt like lead. In fact her
whole body felt heavy, and very, very weak.

'Kate, it's all right . . . You're quite safe.'

Safe! Unexpectedly she shuddered, her eyes
flying open as panic hit her.

She was in the guest-room, in Dominic's bed,
in fact, and he was crouching down beside the
bed, his eyes almost on a level with her own.
Urgency overwhelmed everything else as she

reached towards him, tugging on the rough towelling of the robe he was wearing, her voice sharp and high with anxiety.

'Dominic, there's someone downstairs. I heard them . . .' She shuddered again, and then frowned, remembering. 'I saw them . . . I . . .'

'You fainted, Kate. No, it's all right.' He stood up, bending over her, his fingers curling comfortingly round her arm. 'No one's broken in,' he told her reassuringly.

'But . . . but I saw them . . .'

'You saw me, Kate,' he corrected her gently. 'I couldn't sleep and I'd gone to make myself a drink. I'm sorry I frightened you so much.'

Dominic . . . it had been Dominic all the time. She couldn't seem to stop shaking—a physical reaction to the shock, she recognised dizzily.

'When you fainted I brought you in here because this room was the nearest.' His fingers left her arm, and she could have cried, she felt so bereft. He straightened up and in the lamplight that illuminated the room she saw that his legs and chest were bare where they were not covered by his robe.

The knowledge that he was naked beneath it made her stomach twist in aching heat, the blood surging up under her skin.

'I'll go down and make you a cup of tea.'

'No.' She shivered again and closed her eyes. 'Please stay with me, Dominic . . . God, I was so frightened!'

She opened her eyes in time to catch the remorse in his. She felt so extraordinarily weak, as though her whole life had suddenly shifted focus, and all that was important now was that he never left her alone again.

She refused to analyse her feelings, clinging instead to his arm.

'Kate!' His fingers covered her own, gently prising them away, his voice rough but warm. 'You know if you stay here that I'll make love to you.'

Did she know that? Yes, she did, she discovered as her muscles turned to jelly and her flesh to fire.

Her eyes slid away from his. 'I can't go back to my own room now ... I'd never sleep.' She shivered, her voice little more than a whisper before it broke completely as she begged huskily, 'Hold me, Dominic ... please hold me ...'

She couldn't bear to look at him, her body tensing completely as she realised what she had said. Eight years ago she had come to this man and begged him to make love to her. Had she forgotten what had happened then?

She made a movement towards the opposite side of the bed to where Dominic was standing, but it was swiftly arrested as his fingers closed on her arm, and then he was bending over her, his hands framing and imprisoning her face as he looked down at her.

'Kate, what have I done to make you so afraid of me?'

You've made me love you, she screamed silently inside. 'I'm not afraid of *you*.' Her lips framed the words almost before her mind thought them. 'You rejected me once, Dominic,' she reminded him huskily. 'You refused to make love to me ...'

'But I'm not refusing this time.'

She felt his breath against her skin, his mouth

touching hers lightly, coaxing her lips apart. This
was what she wanted . . . this was what she had
been born for. Nothing else mattered. She sighed
softly into his mouth, shivering in voluptuous
pleasure as his hands drifted down her body
removing her cotton nightdress. She knew that he
looked at her, she could feel the warm path of his
eyes as they caressed her body.

Beneath his regard she grew supine, drifting on
a soft swell of pleasure.

She opened her eyes and saw him looking at
her. His skin was flushed like that of a man deep
in the grip of a fever, his eyes glittering febrilely
over her skin.

'Kate!'

The raw need in his voice splintered her
indolence, desire, hot and urgent, leaping through
her. She reached up to him instinctively, her
hands curling inside his robe as she pulled him
down towards her.

Their mouths met and fused in explosive
passion. His hands touched her breasts, finding
their tight peaks and stimulating them to the
point where they ached for the hot possession of
his mouth. Her fingers curled into his hair as she
tugged him down to her arching body, tiny
whimpers of need exploding in her throat.

'Kate . . . Kate . . .'

Her name was a chant he muttered into her skin
as he responded to her need, his mouth fastening
over her nipple and tugging delicately on it.

His robe had slipped off his shoulders and in a
frenzy of pleasure she bent her head to run her
tongue over the hardness of his skin, feeling his

body clench and his control splinter, and the
pressure of his mouth against her breast became
deliciously savage.

Dominic moved, rolling on to his back and
taking her with him, his hands savouring the
fullness of her breasts as his lips caressed the
fragile bones of her shoulders.

'Kate, I want you to touch me. Touch me,
Kate.' He groaned the words into her throat,
making her shudder and ache deep down in the
pit of her stomach. The belt of his robe had come
loose and she reached to free it completely,
holding her breath as the towelling slid free of his
body, quickly averting her head from his nudity.

He reached up, cupping her face with his
hands and turning her head back.

'Look at me, Kate,' he instructed softly. 'I
want you to look at me.'

Inside she was a mass of quivering sensations,
her eyes dark and solemn as she followed the
muscled line of his legs, hard and firm, up to his
thighs, and then stopped.

'Kate.' His voice was gentle, coaxing almost.
'Do you really find me so repulsive that you can't
look at me?'

Her eyes flew to his, and what she saw in them
reminded her that when they had made love
before his body had been partially covered, and
that she had not touched him below the waist.
Her reticence sprang from the fact that Ricky had
never allowed her to see him completely naked,
had hated her touching him.

'Well?'

He was smiling at her, looking perfectly

relaxed and at ease, but at the back of his eyes she could see a tiny trace of apprehension and her love for him immediately overwhelmed her fears.

'I don't find you repulsive,' she told him shakily.

'Then look at me,' he insisted softly. 'I want you to see what you do to me.'

She took a deep breath and let her eyes drift slowly down his body, following the line of black hair that narrowed over his belly and then flared wider. Her breath caught and held, her attention mesmerised by the sheer physical perfection of him. Idiotically she felt tears sting her eyes. He was so . . . so beautiful. She wanted to reach out and touch him. To trace that dark arrowing of hair and . . .

She moved like someone in a dream and then froze as she bent towards him, shocked by what she had been going to do. His hand gripped hers and guided it down to the flat hardness of his stomach.

'Yes, Kate . . . *Yes!*'

He said it harshly, violently almost, her body jerking as her eyes locked with his and saw the febrile topaz glitter of them. He wanted her . . . he desired her . . . *She* had aroused him. It was then that Ricky, and all the inferiority he had made her feel, slipped completely away. Beneath her fingers Dominic's skin burned and tensed, a thick groan of pleasure stifled in his throat as she stroked her fingernail lightly up and then down that enticing line of hair. His body tensed and then shuddered as he reached for her, pulling her down against him, his mouth hot and hard where it touched her skin. Her hand was wedged flat against his thigh and when she moved it

caressingly against him, he shuddered violently
and muttered into her throat, 'Kate . . . Kate. I'll
teach you to torment me!'

She felt him move, dropping her on to the
mattress, his hands sliding from her breasts to her
thighs, his mouth . . . She gasped in shocked
tension as she felt his tongue touch her navel. His
hands curved over her hips and then slid under her,
moving down to cup the soft roundness of her
bottom. He was kneeling between her thighs, and
the sudden conviction of what he was going to do
brought a thick choking gasp of denial to her throat
and her body tensed as she struggled wildly to sit
up.

She saw him move . . . felt his mouth on the
inside of her thigh, shocked by the swift surge of
pleasure rushing through her. Ignoring her
frantic struggles to break free, he continued to
caress the quivering vulnerability of her inner
thighs. Torn between pleasure and shock, Kate
felt herself weakening. It was like falling
headlong into deep water and then discovering an
unsuspected current carrying her swiftly to that
high place where it fell in a powerful waterfall. In
this case the current was her own fast building
desire and the waterfall . . . She stiffened as she
felt Dominic's tongue slide moistly against her,
appalled by the intensity of her pleasure. She
wanted to rebuff him and she wanted . . . Oh, God,
she wanted him to go on doing what he was doing
now more than she had wanted anything in her life.

Her tensed muscles relaxed, sobs of pleasure
rising in her throat, her head thrashing frantically
from side to side as she felt his mouth against her,

demanding that she abandon herself to him completely, demanding that she give way to the fierce
surges of pleasure already exploding inside her.

Afterwards he held her trembling body in his
arms, soothing her with soft kisses. She could
taste her body on his mouth; the intimacy of what
he had done to her still half shocking her. In a
way she almost resented the pleasure he had
given her. It made her feel too vulnerable. *He*
made her feel vulnerable.

She only realised she had said the last sentence
out loud when he said huskily to her, 'You have
exactly the same effect on me, you know, Kate.'
She felt him smile, laughter lightening his voice
as he added, 'Or at least, you could have.'

She still hadn't touched him, at least not
properly, and as though he sensed the direction of
her thoughts he asked quietly, 'What is it about my
body that you find so off-putting, Kate?'

'Nothing.' It was the truth, and knowing that
something more was called for she added, 'Ricky
didn't like me to . . .'

'I don't give a damn what Ricky did or did not
like,' Dominic interrupted harshly, leaning over
her. His voice softened and became faintly hoarse
as he muttered, 'I *want* you to touch me . . . I
*need* you to touch me.' He moved slightly,
whether by accident or design she did not know,
and she felt the male hardness of him pressing
into her skin. His hand touched her breast,
cupping it lightly, his mouth moist and pleasur-
able as it moved over her sensitised skin. His lips
nuzzled her breasts, making fresh desire burn up
inside her. Her hands clung to his skin, shaping

the long muscles of his back, and then suddenly, eagerly, joyously moving over his body.

When her hand closed over the erect maleness of him she felt a tiny thrill of pleasure at his shuddering response. His arms held her hard against his body, his mouth fastening over hers, the guttural sounds of pleasure stifled in his throat, freeing her from her last constraints.

When his mouth left hers, she started to scatter tiny, feverish kisses over his skin, letting her senses guide her, giving in completely to the desire to submerge herself completely in her love.

When her mouth touched his stomach, he tensed and then arched against her, muttering feverish words of praise into the heavy air, his fingers reaching down to curl into her hair, shudder after shudder of pleasure ripping through his body as passion rode her, making her move blindly against his body until her mouth found the rigid hardness of him.

When he dragged her away to roll her on to her back and enter her with swift fierceness, she welcomed each primitive thrust of his body, matching them with a complementary rhythm of her own.

He took her swiftly to a shattering climax, crying out her name as pleasure overwhelmed him.

The last thing Kate could remember before she fell asleep was the comforting pressure of his arm, drawing her back into the warmth of his recumbent body.

When she woke up Dominic's arm was still there, and Kate's skin burned as she remembered the previous night. Fear coiled deep inside her, poised to strike like a venomous serpent. What had she done? What had she betrayed to him with her feverish, frantic lovemaking? She was petrified that he might have guessed the truth; that he might know now that she loved him. She had to escape. She couldn't endure the humiliation of facing him if he knew.

Frantically she managed to wriggle free of his arm and slide out of the bed. He was still deeply asleep, his face agonisingly youthful, his dark hair ruffled. She had dislodged the duvet as she moved and it had slid down his body, leaving him bare to the hips. Here and there on his skin Kate could see the faint marks of her own teeth, and she shuddered in shocked denial of the intensity of her passion. It did not matter that her own body bore the same marks, or that Dominic's passion had been as great as her own. He was not vulnerable as she was. . . . All he had felt was desire, while she . . .

Why not stay . . . why not stay and see if she couldn't change that desire into love? The violence with which she shuddered away from the mere thought brought her up against a truth she had tried desperately to hide away from. She was still frightened of Dominic's rejection. She tried to dismiss it, but the knowledge would not go away. While Dominic slept she hurried into her own room, grabbing clothes at random and stuffing them into a holdall. She had to get away . . . she had to . . . if she stayed here . . . But where could she go?

Harry and Liz—she had an open invitation to stay with them. No one would know where she was. Dominic could not trace her to them.

After last night she knew that his desire of her was strong enough to make his pursuit of her relentness, at least while that desire lasted. But how long would it last? Not as long as her love. Why not stay . . . take what he has to offer and worry about it ending when it ends? a traitorous voice whispered, but Kate pushed it away. She couldn't live like that every day a torment of wondering if this was going to be the one when he looked at her without desire and then coldly turned his back on her. No . . . better to make a clean break now.

Right up until she had driven the car on to the main road she had expected Dominic to wake up and come after her. Her chest was aching from holding her breath, her body tight with apprehension and pain.

Liz welcomed her placidly, explaining that Harry had gone out. 'You've been having quite a lot of excitement over your way,' she commented to Kate as she made her a cup of coffee. 'Caught them yet, have they?'

Kate shook her head. She had already asked Liz if she might stay with them for a few days, using as an excuse the fact that she needed to consult Harry about her new commission. Liz hadn't said so, but Kate suspected that the older woman wasn't deceived, but if so, she was far too placid and compassionate to question her further.

Harry, though, was not so reticent.

He arrived an hour later, and having welcomed Kate with a warm hug asked her what had brought her down to see them. She gave him the same explanation she had given Liz, and his eyebrows rose slightly. 'I thought you were quite satisfied with the way it's going,' he commented, adding shrewdly, 'I think you're hiding something, Kate, but if you are, that's your business. Just remember, you can't go on running for the rest of your life.'

Liz had left them on their own, and now Kate's cheeks coloured hotly. 'Just what makes you think I'm running?' she demanded crossly. 'Honestly, Harry . . .!' and then to her own consternation she burst into tears.

She had never felt so mortified in her entire life. She was twenty-seven years old, for God's sake, and here she was bursting into tears like an adolescent.

Twenty-seven or not, it was sheer bliss to put her head on Harry's shoulder and sob out her misery. Her father had never been a physically affectionate person, although she had known that he cared about her, and Ricky of course had made it more than clear how little physical contact he wanted with her. That, coupled with her mother's defection, had ensured that her life had been lamentably short of people to lean on, and it said much for her emotional state that she was now actually doing so.

Harry waited until the sobs had subsided into muffled hiccups interspersed with words of apology, before handing her a handkerchief and saying easily, 'Mop up, then we'll both have a drink and talk this through.' He saw her face and grinned at her. 'You forget, Kate, I've had two daughters of my own. I know what it's all about.'

Feeling remarkably weak-minded, Kate allowed him to propel her into the small sitting-room where he poured them both a drink.

'Liz will wonder . . .' But she broke off when Harry shook his head.

'She won't wonder anything,' he told her firmly. 'She told me when I came in that you were upset about something . . . or rather, perhaps, someone. Care to talk about it, Kate?'

Unbelievably she did. It was as though all the self-control that had held her together for so many years had completely disintegrated following Dominic's reappearance in her life. She forced herself to go back to the beginning, telling Harry briefly about her marriage . . . twisting the whisky tumbler tensely in her fingers as she did so, and then hurriedly taking a nerve-strengthening gulp before telling him about her attempt to seduce Dominic.

Her eyes were on the glass she was holding so she didn't see the compassion in his eyes as he looked at her downbent head. Poor Kate, always so calm and self-controlled, but inwardly a mass of tensions and fears. Some men oughtn't to be allowed near any woman, he thought, listening to her, but he kept silent, letting her go all through her story.

'And so . . . you've run away from him,' he said quietly, when she had finished. 'But why, Kate? He wants you . . . you want him . . .'

'I love him,' she corrected bitterly. 'And I ran away because I'm afraid, Harry. I can't forget that he's already rejected me once . . . that he hated me, resented me . . .'

'I doubt that, Kate.'

She looked up to see Harry shaking his head. 'You say he's told you that he couldn't make love to

you the first time, even though he wanted you,
because you were his friend's wife. The type of man
driven by compulsive desire and hatred of that
desire doesn't react like that, Kate . . . I think you'll
find if you asked him that he hated himself.'

'But he thought . . .' Her mouth trembled and
she went on, 'He thought I was sleeping around
with everyone I could find. He despised me,
Harry . . . and now suddenly he's saying he wants
me. I can't trust that kind of turnaround. All the
time I'm with him I'm tense . . . waiting for the
axe to fall, so to speak, and for him to tell me it's
all been a trick, that he doesn't want me at all.'

To her chagrin, Harry grinned, his eyes
twinkling as he said drolly, 'From what you've said
to me I surmise that he's already demonstrated
most definitely that he does want you, Kate . . . and
that's something it's very difficult for a man to fake
. . . but I know what you mean.' He became more
sober. 'I can see that he's used his image of you as a
means of defence against wanting you, but you
can't blame him for that. Men are very territorial
animals, my dear, even in this day and age. Very
few of them can tolerate sharing what they believe
to be theirs. Now I'm not going to argue the pros
and cons of that with you. I'm simply stating a fact,
but are you sure it's just him you're running from,
Kate, and not yourself as well?'

She tensed and looked sharply at him,
demanding huskily, 'What do you mean?'

'I mean, my dear, that you say you love him,
but it's obvious that you resent feeling that way
about him. You don't *want* to love him, do you?'

Kate frowned. 'No. No, I don't . . . it makes

me feel too vulnerable,' she burst out impulsively. 'It frightens me, Harry.' She hugged her arms round her body, suddenly looking very forlorn and young.

'Then you should understand how he feels, shouldn't you?'

Her head came up sharply, her eyes widening.

'Most human beings are by nature defensive, Kate,' Harry told her softly. 'Sometimes we have to put aside our defences and be open to others. Will he be able to trace you here?'

She shook her head.

'Well then, if you do love him . . . if you really want him, I suggest you go back and talk to him. He may not be able to love you . . . but isn't it better to face the truth than to keep on running?'

Was it?

Kate didn't know. And she didn't feel any closer to knowing the next morning when she woke up, thoroughly disorientated by the unfamiliar bedroom until she remembered where she was and why.

The day dragged, even though Harry and Liz did their best to keep her entertained, and at last after dinner that evening she made her decision. Getting up abruptly from the settee where she had been sitting with Liz watching television, she announced,

'I'm going back.'

From his easy chair Harry smiled at her. 'Good girl,' he said quietly.

They both saw her off, Harry coming up to her car window to say gently, 'Remember, whatever happens, Kate, there's no shame in loving someone honestly. It's when we try to be dishonest to ourselves that the problems start.'

The closer she got to the village the more her tension increased. It was all right for Harry to say stop running and tell him the truth, but now, suddenly, she didn't know how she was going to face Dominic. Or even if he would want her to face him. He might already have left the village. He might be in London—anywhere . . .

Remember he's looking for a house in the area, a calming inner voice interceded. But what if he wouldn't see her . . . what if . . . Clamping down on her tumultuous thoughts, she slowed down as she drove through the village. It was already dusk and she intended to go straight to bed when she got home. Tomorrow she might feel braver about talking to Dominic. She certainly hoped so.

She drove carefully round what she knew to be an extremely bad bend, and then braked sharply as she saw what lay in front of her. On the opposite side of the road, its bonnet embedded in a low stone wall, was a large BMW. Behind it were parked two police cars, lights flashing. A huddle of men in uniform were grouped round the crashed car. It looked oddly familiar—and then sickeningly Kate realised why. It was Dominic's car.

There was a singing noise in her ears, a dull roaring in her blood. Dear God! She mustn't faint. Somehow she managed to stagger out of the car and across to the group of men. One of them turned at her approach.

'What . . .? What happened?' she stammered sickly.

'Bad accident, miss.' The policeman's voice was calm and soothing.

'Was . . . was anyone hurt?' She was shivering violently now and she could see the man frowning slightly.

'The driver was killed.' It was one of the other men who spoke, his voice blunt, carrying an edge of disapproval.

Killed . . . Killed . . . Dominic was dead. Somehow Kate managed to get back in her car and get it started, even though she heard the policeman calling something out to her. No doubt he had been aware of her shock, but she didn't want to answer any questions now . . . all she wanted to do was to be alone with this enormous unbelievable pain that was flowering inside her.

Dead . . . dead . . . dead . . . The words beat out a monotonous rhythm in her brain all the way home, as though somehow by repetition they might become real. But it was real. Dominic was dead. He had died at the wheel of his car. Doing what? Looking for her. She stalled the car as she brought it to a halt in the drive, her body so weak that she could barely walk to the front door. Everything seemed to be swaying round her, a terrible draining weakness taking her over, almost as though her life-blood was draining from her body.

Automatically she made for the drawing-room, pushing open the door and then coming to an abrupt halt as a figure detached itself from one of the easy chairs.

'So you're back. Where the hell have you been?'

Dominic? Kate swayed weakly on legs that threatened to crumple beneath her. 'But you . . . you're dead . . .' She stared at him, trembling wildly, unable to strand the strain of two consecutive shocks coming so quickly on top of one another.

'Dead? Wishful thinking, I'm afraid, my pet.'
His voice was hatefully sardonic, his movements
as he came towards her banishing her first dread
that she was simply conjuring up his memory in
her anguish. She tried to breathe and found that
her muscles simply refused to work, her eyes
growing wide as she stared and stared into his face.
When he reached her she stretched out blindly, her
fingers trembling as she touched his face.

'Kate . . .' His voice was rough, his eyes
impatient as he grabbed her hands and tugged
them down to her sides. 'Just what the hell are
you playing at? God, I never know where the hell
I am with you! What is it you want from me?
Revenge . . . is that it? You want to pay me back
for rejecting you, is that it?'

Kate heard him, but the words didn't register,
she was still trying to come to terms with the fact
that he was alive.

'You're not dead.' She repeated the words
slowly, still staring at him. 'You're not dead . . .'
She kept on saying it, her body trembling more
intensely with each repetition.

'Kate?'

Dominic released her hands, cupping her face
and turning it slightly so that the light fell
sharply on her white tortured features. Kate felt
him draw in his breath.

She closed her eyes, feeling the horror recede. 'I
saw your car . . . the BMW. The police were
there. I asked them if anyone was hurt, and they
told me . . . They told me you were dead.'

Her control broke over the last few words,

huge sobs shaking her body.

Above her she heard Dominic swear, and then she was being rocked against his body, his arms wrapped tightly round her. 'Not me, my darling,' he soothed her. 'Not me . . . the prisoners who escaped took it. I've been driving all over the place looking for you, and foolishly when I went down to the cottage to check it earlier I left the keys in it. They must have seen me arrive. It didn't get them very far. The driver was killed and the other man badly injured. The police have only just left here.'

Gradually her body ceased to shake, control returning to her limbs and her mind. Harry had been right; it was time to stop running.

'Why did you run away?'

She could feel the tension in his body and she knew that no matter what the outcome she had to tell him the truth.

Lifting her head so that she could look into his eyes, she said quietly, 'Because I love you . . . because I was frightened . . . because . . .'

Dominic didn't let her get any further, his eyes suddenly darkening with a mixture of emotions she found it hard to define.

'You love me?' Incredulity and anger seemed to be blended in his voice in equal parts, and for a moment she wished she had not told him, but it was too late for that now.

'Yes . . .'

'You *love* me and you let me think . . . You let me think it was just physical, just an eight-year-old ache that needed easing. Damn you, Kate . . .' His voice thickened over the last few words and then she was hauled against him, his mouth punishingly fierce as it fastened over her own.

It took her several seconds to recognise his near-violence as passion and not anger, and then easily and joyously her mouth opened beneath his, her arms going round his neck. Without breaking the kiss, he shifted slightly so that she was balanced against his body, aware of its hard, exciting pulsing.

Tiny prickles of excitement burned her skin, her need to feel the life force of him deep inside her after believing that it was lost to her for ever overriding everything else. Her hand moved to the waistband of his jeans and slid down over his thigh.

'No ...' Dominic's hand clamped down over her own, turning her eyes brilliant with shock. 'Not yet,' he amended softly. 'First we have to talk. Do you *know* what you've put me through?' he demanded, almost shaking her. 'I couldn't believe it when I woke up and you'd gone!'

'I couldn't stay, knowing you only ... only desired me,' she mumbled, her tongue suddenly thick and cumbersome, tripping up the words.

'Only desire you?' He *did* shake her now, muffling a tiny sound of despair against her throat. 'Kate, why on earth are you so blind?' he asked throatily. 'I do desire you ... but I also love you. I fell in love with you the moment I saw you. Surely you realised that?'

He saw the incredulity and disbelief dawn in her eyes and then give way to shining joy, and laughed unsteadily.

'You little fool! Why on *earth* did you think I was so savage with you? Why do you think I haven't touched another woman in eight years? Why do you think I keep coming after you, letting you slap me down, letting you torment me until I'm way, way out of control? Not just because I desire you.'

'I thought you hated me ... despised me ...' Her voice was a dry rasp.

'I despised myself,' Dominic told her wryly. 'Firstly for wanting another man's wife to the point where I was on the verge of forgetting all the rules I'd lived my life by, to make love to her, and secondly for being stupid enough to fall crazily in love with an adolescent nymphomaniac ... I told myself it made it easier to keep away from you, believing that you slept around, but it didn't. It just drove me crazy, imagining all the men who were getting what I'd denied myself. When I found out Vera and Ian were moving into this area, I knew it was fate. I knew I'd see you again. When I discovered you were a widow, I told myself that now I would have a chance to get you out of my blood for all time ... that if I made love to you, it would conquer this fever for you that had dominated me for so long. But long before I touched you, long before Sue told me the truth, I knew it wasn't so ... I knew then that I loved you. Do you believe me?'

As she looked into the topaz depths of his eyes Kate knew that she did.

'Yes,' she told him quietly, trembling as he raised her palm to his mouth, lacing his fingers with hers, his tongue brushing the delicate skin.

'Let's put the past behind us, Kate, and have a fresh start ... as man and wife. And this time I promise you your marriage will be everything that a marriage should be . . . Well?'

His voice was soft, but there was no mistaking the tension holding his body, or the anxiety in his eyes.

He did love her. Impossibly against all the odds they had found one another, and he was right, it was time to forget the past. In order to face the future she had to take him on trust, in just the same way that he had to trust her. Kate recognised that now.

'Yes . . .' She said it quietly, and then more fiercely, pressing her body against the length of his and lifting her mouth for his kiss.

His breathing was thready . . . erratic.

'If I kiss you now, the way I want to, I won't be able to stop until I've made love to you. God, Kate . . .' He groaned in protest as she moved her hips wantonly against his. Beads of sweat stood out on his skin, his arousal hard and hot against her, reluctant laughter breaking through the passion darkening his eyes as she stroked her fingers suggestively over the tight fabric of his jeans.

'Kate . . .' Dominic's voice held a warning, but she ignored it, excitement trembling through her as he said her name again on a rougher note and then bent to pick her up.

At the top of the stairs he paused and looked down into her face to say rawly, 'I love you, Kate, and I'm never, ever going to let you forget it. Do you hear that?'

She heard, and best of all she believed. She had come through pain and fear to be at this point in her life with this man. She looked at him with her heart in her eyes and said softly, 'I hear.'

# Harlequin Presents

## Coming Next Month

**967 THE DECEPTION TRAP Ann Charlton**
Tess is no ordinary maid. She's merely posing as one to embarrass an Australian business tycoon—to repay him for deserting her family when their fortunes fell years ago. But everything backfires.

**968 TOO DANGEROUS TO LOVE Sandra Clark**
When her aunt dies, a young Welsh woman presumes she'll inherit the family fabric-printing workshop. Instead, it goes to the son of her aunt's ex-lover. And his claim extends to more than the business !

**969 TO SPEAK OF LOVE Claudia Jameson**
A merchant banker's brotherly guidance was invaluable to a neglected teenager in Madrid but must be discounted now that she's old enough to know in her heart what's right for her.

**970 PASSIONATE CHOICE Flora Kidd**
An Englishwoman, searching for sunken artifacts in the Caribbean with her fiancé, feels seasick when she meets their dive ship captain—the man who betrayed her love three years ago.

**971 HEAT OF THE NIGHT Charlotte Lamb**
Bitter from the discovery that her fiancé was a first-class heel, a woman flees to Florence where she meets a man who's dynamic and charming—perhaps too charming to trust?

**972 FANTASY WOMAN Annabel Murray**
Fantasy Woman, the masked star of England's popular show that makes wishes come true, is less successful with her own dreams. Until Tod Fallon appears to fulfill her wish by making her fall in love with him.

**973 JUNGLE ISLAND Kay Thorpe**
When a young Englishwoman journeys to Brunei to fulfill her late father's last request, she has to brave the jungle—along with her growing passion for the rugged seaman who guides her to her destination.

**974 CAGE OF ICE Sally Wentworth**
To shield her married sister from kidnappers, Domino takes her place in the Austrian Alps. But her own heart is held ransom when she falls in love with her bodyguard and can't tell him she's not a married woman.

Available in April wherever paperback books are sold, or through Harlequin Reader Service:

In the U.S.
P.O. Box 1397
Buffalo, N.Y.
14240-1397

in Canada
P.O. Box 603
Fort Erie, Ontario
L2A 5X3

For the millions who can't read
Give the Gift of Literacy

**One out of five adults in North America
cannot read or write well enough
to fill out a job application
or understand the directions on a bottle of medicine.**

**You can change all this by joining the fight
against illiteracy.**

For more information write to:
Contact, Box 81826, Lincoln, Neb. 68501
In the United States, call toll free: 800-228-3225

**The only degree you need
is a degree of caring**

"This ad made possible with the cooperation of the Coalition for Literacy and the Ad Council."
Give the Gift of Literacy Campaign is a project of the book and periodical industry,
in partnership with Telephone Pioneers of America.

LIT—A—1